"Do You ██████ Taggart A██████

"Not exactly," Beck█ ███████
one," she added fir██ ████
Miz Albright than K█zy ████ or that lady
at the rodeo."

"What makes you think you'll get any of them?"

"The way you look at them."

Taggart felt a flush crawl up his neck. "How do I look at them?"

"Like you want 'em," Becky said bluntly. "The way I looked at dogs before I got Digger."

Taggart rubbed a hand down his face. He looked like he wanted a woman? *That* was why his daughter hadn't been doing her schoolwork? *That* was why she had been following Felicity Albright around town? *That* was why she was wearing spurs to school? So he could meet her teacher and—

And what? Bed Felicity Albright? He didn't think that would have occurred to Becky.

Then what? *Marry her?*

Taggart groaned and closed his eyes.

Dear Reader,

Cowboys and cops...sexy men with a swagger...just the kind of guys to make your head turn. *That's* what we've got for you this month in Silhouette Desire.

The romance begins when Taggart Jones meets his match in Anne McAllister's wonderful MAN OF THE MONTH, *The Cowboy and the Kid.* This is the latest in her captivating CODE OF THE WEST miniseries. And the fun continues with Mitch Harper in *A Gift for Baby,* the next book in Raye Morgan's THE BABY SHOWER series.

Cindy Gerard has created a dynamic hero in the *very* masculine form of J. D. Hazzard in *The Bride Wore Blue,* book #1 in the NORTHERN LIGHTS BRIDES series. And if rugged rascals are your favorite, don't miss Jake Spencer in Dixie Browning's *The Baby Notion,* which is book #1 of DADDY KNOWS LAST, Silhouette's new cross-line continuity. (Next month, look for Helen R. Myers's *Baby in a Basket* as DADDY KNOWS LAST continues in Silhouette Romance!)

Gavin Cantrell is sure to weaken your knees in *Gavin's Child* by Caroline Cross, part of the delightful BACHELORS AND BABIES promotion. And Jackie Merritt—along with hero Duke Sheridan—kicks off her MADE IN MONTANA series with *Montana Fever.*

Heroes to fall in love with—and love scenes that will make your toes curl. That's what Silhouette Desire is all about. Until next month—enjoy!

All the best,

Lucia Macro

Senior Editor

Please address questions and book requests to:
Silhouette Reader Service
U.S.: 3010 Walden Ave., P.O. Box 1325, Buffalo, NY 14269
Canadian: P.O. Box 609, Fort Erie, Ont. L2A 5X3

ANNE McALLISTER

THE COWBOY AND THE KID

SILHOUETTE *Desire*

Published by Silhouette Books

America's Publisher of Contemporary Romance

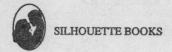

SILHOUETTE BOOKS

ISBN 0-373-76009-4

THE COWBOY AND THE KID

Books by Anne McAllister

Silhouette Desire

*Cowboys Don't Cry #907
*Cowboys Don't Quit #944
*Cowboys Don't Stay #969
*The Cowboy and the Kid #1009

*Code of the West

ANNE McALLISTER

was born and raised in California, land of surfers, swimmers and beach-volleyball players. She spent her teenage years researching them in hopes of finding the perfect hero. It turned out, however, that a few summer weeks spent at her grandparents' in Colorado and all those hours in junior high spent watching Robert Fuller playing Jess Harper on "Laramie" were formative. She was fixated on dark, handsome, intense, lone-wolf types. Twenty-nine years ago she found the perfect one prowling the stacks of the university library and married him. They now have four children, three dogs, a fat cat and live in the Midwest (as in "Is this heaven?" "No, it's Iowa.") in a reasonable facsimile of semiperfect wedded bliss to which she always returns— even though the last time she was in California she had lunch with Robert Fuller.

The fifth installment of CODE OF THE WEST— Jed McCall's story—will be coming to you in *Cowboy Pride*—only from Silhouette Desire.

For Grace Green
who knows about heroes called Taggart

For Nan Welch
who makes third grade at least as much fun as work

And most especially for Brett Leffew
who makes riding a bull look easy
and doing research a joy
This one's for you

Prologue

From the Scrapbook of *Taggart W. Jones*

JONES BOY BUSTS MUTTON AT RODEO

Taggart Jones, 5, son of Will and Gaye Jones of rural Elmer, won the mutton-busting event at the Wilsall Rodeo last weekend....

JONES STEER-RIDING CHAMP

Taggart Jones, 12-year-old son of Gaye and Will Jones of rural Elmer, took first place in the junior steer riding in Billings last weekend. He rode Buckminster for a score of 82.

TAGGART JONES WINS BULL RIDING AT HIGH SCHOOL FINALS RODEO

Taggart Jones, 17, of rural Elmer, took top bull-riding honors at the National High School Rodeo with an 81-point ride to cap a successful week. He didn't buck off once.

JONES GETS HIS FIRST NFR BERTH

(AP) Taggart Jones, 22, of rural Elmer, Montana, 12th place finisher in the year's PRCA bull-riding standings last month, will go to the National Finals Rodeo in Las Vegas which begins tomorrow. Only the top 15 cowboys in each event will ride in ten performances over the next week to determine the world champion in each event.

JONES HAS WEEKEND TO REMEMBER AT FRISCO COW PALACE

It wasn't enough to win both the average and the top-scoring 91 point bull ride at San Francisco's famous Cow Palace Rodeo last weekend. No, Taggart Jones had to become a father, too.

"I wasn't expecting it," the new dad told reporters as he grinned from ear to ear. "Not yet, anyway. The baby wasn't due for another two weeks. I was hoping to get home before she did."

But seven-pound Rebecca Kathleen Jones couldn't wait to congratulate her daddy, who is on his way home right now, bringing a shiny buckle to his brand-new daughter, with the promise of more to come. Eighth in the world as of last Sunday's ride, Jones will be competing in his 3rd NFR in Las Vegas next month.

Becky will undoubtly be there to cheer him on.

ON THE ROAD AGAIN...WITH KID IN TOW

Taggart Jones, 24, and Noah Tanner, 28, two of the PRCA's top rough-stock cowboys, have a new traveling partner. She's got light brown hair and big green eyes, and, no, she's not a barrel racer. The lady is Taggart's three-month-old daughter, Becky.

Born the weekend her father won at the Cow Palace, Becky spent her sixth-week birthday in Las Vegas at the NFR watching as Daddy took 3rd. They spent Christmas at home in Montana and missed the Denver Stock Show because "she still had a little bit of colic."

But now that colic is a thing of the past, Becky, her dad and her honorary uncle, Noah Tanner, are heading back down the road.

"My folks offered to take her," said Taggart, a divorced dad, "But she's my kid. They raised me. Now it's up to me to raise Becky."

Already smiling at three months, Becky could tell you that—with a little help from his cowboy friends— her daddy is doing a fine job so far.

ME AND MY DAD

BY
BECKY

Sept. 23

Dear Mr. Jones,

Becky has won our "Student of the Week"
award for first grade. She is so clever and
innovative—a delight to have in class!

Mrs. Ward

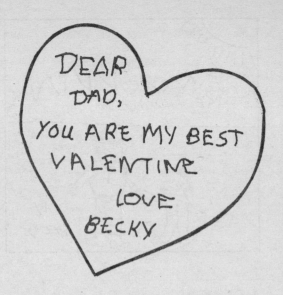

DEAR DAD,

YOU ARE MY BEST VALENTINE

LOVE BECKY

JONES WINS GOLD AT NFR!

Taggart Jones, 30, six-time finalist at the PRCA National Finals Rodeo, won the bull-riding championship yesterday at the Thomas and Mack Arena in Las Vegas, Nevada.

The Elmer, Montana, native lasted the full eight seconds on nine of the ten bulls he rode during the week-long December rodeo.

NFR CHAMPS INJURED IN STORM, BOTH GRAVE

LARAMIE, Wy. (AP) New PRCA world champions, bull-rider Taggart Jones, 30, and bronc-rider Noah Tanner, 34, were seriously injured last evening when a semi veered out of control on Interstate 80 west of Laramie and slammed into their van.

Jones, a native of Montana, and Tanner, of Colorado, were on their way home from the National Finals Rodeo in Las Vegas, where on Sunday each won the world champion title in his event. The driver of the semi was trying to pass on the snow-covered highway when he hit Tanner's van.

Jones, who has had a relatively injury-free bull-riding career, suffered a severe concussion and broken leg. He was taken unconscious from the vehicle and has still not regained consciousness.

Tanner, despite an injury-plagued career, has made the National Finals seven times, finally winning this year. He received a punctured lung, broken ribs, and injuries to his wrist, shoulder and knee in the accident.

Dear Daddy

Gramma says you will be home before ore you get this, but I want to write it so you can see it when you are in bed getting well and I am at school. It's so you will ~~no~~ kno I am thinking of you when I am not with you because I kno you think of me. Maybe when you are better you will take me with you next time. I do miss you. I wouldn't miss school.

love,
Becky

TAGGART JONES RETIRES

Reigning PRCA champion bull rider, Taggart Jones, 30, of Elmer, Montana, announced his retirement from rodeo yesterday in Bozeman. Citing his desire to spend time with his six-year-old daughter, Jones hung up his spurs.

Seriously hurt last December when the van he was riding in was hit by a semi during a snowstorm the day after the NFR, Jones denied that his injuries were the determining factor.

"They made me think, though," he admitted. "I'm the only parent Becky's got. I have nothing left to prove as far as bull-riding is concerned. She's only six, so I still have a ways to go as a dad."

Jones and his traveling partner, now business associate, bronc-riding champ Noah Tanner, who also retired last week, will be keeping their hand in the rodeo circuit, though, grooming their successors. They're opening a bull- and bronc-riding school on the Jones ranch west of Elmer and hope to be operational by June.

One

Having a father was a big responsibility.

Becky Jones knew that better than almost anyone. She'd been taking care of her own father by herself—except for now and then, when Grandma and Grandpa and her dad's best friend, Noah, lent a hand—since she was two months old, and she'd be eight in October. That was a long while.

Taggart—that was his name—was a pretty low-maintenance dad most of the time. He was thirty-two years old and in good health except for the pins in his knee and the occasional twinge left over from his bull-riding days. He didn't yell a lot or smoke or spit or chew—which was better than most of the dads she knew. He took off his boots when he came in the house; he washed the dishes almost every night; he kept his room pretty neat and he let her make a mess in hers.

Also, he'd been around since she was born, and that was a big plus as far as Becky was concerned.

It was certainly more than her best friend, Susannah, could say. Susannah's dad, Noah, hadn't even known he had a daughter until almost two years ago!

That seemed pretty careless to Becky, but she could hardly talk since her own mother didn't get any prizes in the responsibility department. She'd got fed up and left Becky and her dad more than seven years ago and had never come back.

At least once he knew Susannah existed, Noah Tanner had stuck around. He was even married to Susannah's mother now. Susannah said he and Tess, her mom, were in love. Becky guessed they must be because they'd had another baby—a boy called Clay—right after Christmas last year and were going to have another baby this November! Pretty soon Susannah would have lots of brothers and sisters to share the responsibility with. With *two* parents, you'd probably need that.

Becky, however, was on her own.

Until two years ago that hadn't been a problem. Before she started going to school full-time, Becky had gone down the road with Taggart from rodeo to rodeo, and she'd done a pretty good job taking care of him and keeping him out of trouble. Other cowboys got drunk and chased girls and raised heck, but not her dad.

"Taggart's getting pretty settled these days," her grandpa often said.

And her grandma always nodded and ruffled Becky's hair. "And we know why, don't we?" she would say, smiling at her granddaughter. "Because of you. You take such good care of your dad."

But she couldn't prevent the accident. She hadn't even been with him at the time.

She'd started first grade that fall and had stayed with her grandparents while Taggart had gone down the road without her. Becky thought that was dumb. She'd always learned a lot going down the road. Hadn't she learned to read by sounding out the letters on road signs? Couldn't she follow a map almost as good as he could? But arguing was useless. Sometimes her dad was as stubborn as the bulls he rode. She'd had to go to school anyway, and he'd traveled with Noah all that fall.

Noah hadn't been able to prevent the accident, either.

It had happened in December almost two years ago, right after the National Finals Rodeo. Becky remembered how mad she'd been because she couldn't even go to that—she'd *always* gone to the finals with him!

But he'd said, no, school was more important. Becky disagreed, and she'd intended to tell him in no uncertain terms—after she gave him a big hug.

On the day he was due to arrive she'd bounced out of bed early, wondering if maybe he was already waiting downstairs to surprise her. It would be just like him to get here early. She knew he missed her as much as she missed him. Besides, he was bringing her a big gold buckle this time because he was the new champion bull rider of the world! Naturally he'd be in a hurry for her to see it.

She'd rushed to pull on her jeans and shirt, buttoning it wrong and not even stopping to do it over, so eager was she to race down the stairs and leap into his arms.

He wasn't there. Only Grandma and Grandpa were in the kitchen, standing real stiff as they looked at her. Then Grandpa had come over and put his hands on her shoulders.

"There's been an accident, Beck," he told her in a low quiet voice, the one he used when he was gentling his horses. Becky thought he looked the way he had when the foal of his best mare, Cedar, died last spring. "A truck hit Noah's van in the snowstorm. Your dad's in the hospital in Laramie."

"Hospital?" Becky knew all about hospitals. That was where they'd taken her great-grandma before she'd died. It was where old Mr. Ennis had gone, too, and she remembered them burying him last Fourth of July. It was also where her friend Tuck McCall's mother had been. She was dead now, too.

Becky felt like the time Tuck had hit her in the stomach with his football. Only worse. A million, trillion times worse.

Her father wasn't dead, they told her. He was in a coma. That was like sleeping, Grandma said. Only sometimes, Tuck told her later—which nobody else would—you didn't wake up.

All the time her dad was in the coma, Becky had had that football feeling.

"He'll be all right, you'll see," her grandma had told her over and over. But Becky had seen the fear in her grandmother's eyes and knew Grandma had the football feeling, too.

The next afternoon they said he woke up. Becky wasn't sure she'd have believed it—even though her grandma was laughing and crying at the same time—except Grandma held the phone out so Becky could talk to him.

"D-Daddy?"

"Hey, Pard." He sounded awful, like he'd swallowed Grandpa's chew. But it was him; nobody else ever called her Pard.

She breathed again. "Daddy." The football feeling was gone. She felt like she could fly.

"Sorry I missed your program, Pard."

As if she cared about a dumb old Christmas program. "When are you comin' home, Daddy? Soon?"

"Soon."

"For Christmas?"

"You'd better believe it. They're not keepin' me one minute longer than they have to. You can come and get me, okay?"

"'Kay." She gripped the receiver tightly, the way she would hang on to his neck if he were here. She listened to him breathing. It was the best sound she'd ever heard.

"Love you, Pard," he said at last.

"Love you, too."

Her grandma took the phone back then. Becky ran out to the barn and climbed up on the top rail of Cedar's stall to press her face into the sorrel's mane. There, for the first time since she'd heard about the accident, Becky cried.

Sometimes, if she thought about it now, she could get scared all over again. She knew it had scared her dad, too. Once he got better, Taggart said he wasn't ever leaving her again. He and Noah decided that going down the road was just too hard on family men. They were both world champions. They'd proved all they needed to prove.

So they started a bull- and bronc-riding school. Grandpa had the stock, and Taggart and Noah had the know-how. Now, a year and a half later, it was up and running.

Noah and Tess and Susannah had just finished building a house down the road. Becky and Taggart had lived with Grandma and Grandpa while he and Noah got things going. But three months ago, Grandpa and Grandma had decided to try "city life" and bought a house in Bozeman, leaving Becky and her father on their own.

Most of the time they were fine, just the two of them.

But sometimes, lately she wasn't sure.

This past summer, for example, when they'd gone down to the rodeo in Cheyenne, and he'd been trying to win her a stuffed bear in the shooting gallery, he'd missed five times! Not because he wasn't a good shot. But because instead of looking at the target, he was busy watching some lady with tight jeans and long blond hair!

Becky's company hadn't been enough the day they went over to the rodeo in Missoula, either. He spent so much time talking to that barrel racer from Oregon that he didn't realize how much soda pop and candy Becky had eaten. She'd been sick all night.

She'd thought maybe he was just distracted when they were traveling. She knew her grandpa had an old saying, something about "keeping them down on the farm...." Becky assumed he meant the ranch, but lately even at the ranch things had been strange.

Like tonight when they were having dinner at Susannah's. Becky and Susannah were playing chopsticks on the piano, and she turned around to see if her dad had noticed how good she was getting. But instead of watching her, he'd been watching Noah kiss Tess. He'd had a funny look on his face, too.

"They're making up for lost time," Susannah explained. "Newlyweds do that." She'd giggled. Becky had, too. Taggart didn't even smile.

Becky left Susannah playing the piano and slid off the bench to go to where he stood propped against the windowsill. She leaned back against his legs and felt his fingers settle on her shoulders and tighten until they almost hurt. She reached a hand back and touched his. His grip eased and his fingers covered hers. His thumb rubbed the back of her hand.

Later that night when they were driving home, she had to ask him three times if she could drive the truck through the gate when he opened and closed it.

"Huh?" he said at last. Then, "Sure, if you want to." But it seemed to Becky as if he'd barely heard. He didn't even tell her what a good job she did when he got back in the truck. He didn't seem to notice at all.

"Are you missing Julie?" she asked him finally when he was tucking her into bed. Her mother, she meant. She never called her Mommy because no one else ever had.

He blinked, then frowned. "Missing Julie? Of course not. What the heck brought that on?"

Becky gave a tiny shrug and scrunched back into the pillow. "Dunno. I just . . . wondered."

He looked at her narrowly. Then he shrugged, too. "Don't be stupid." Then he ruffled her hair and dropped a kiss on her lips. " 'Night, Pard."

Becky's arms came up and locked around his neck, tugging him down for another, harder kiss. " 'Night," she said fiercely.

When he left, he winked at her, and she smiled, thinking she was imagining things and that everything was going to be all right.

But when she woke up a few hours later, she could hear the television on. Unless he was watching cartoons with her or videos of bull rides, Taggart almost never watched TV. Curious, Becky crept downstairs.

He was watching a movie. Not even a car-chase movie, which, as far as she knew, was the only kind he ever watched. On the screen she saw a man and a woman talking, arguing. Talking some more. And then, when the music got really soppy and the lady sniffled and wiped her eyes, they started smiling at each other. And then they were touching. And kissing. A whole lot of kissing.

Taggart flicked the remote. Becky figured he'd shut it off. She was wrong. He played it back and watched it again. And again.

For a long time, even after he shut it off, he didn't move. He just sat there, his hands in his lap, while Becky crouched on the steps, watching. At last, he got up—real slow, like when all his muscles hurt from bull-riding—and walked to the window. He stood with his hands tucked into his pockets staring out into the darkness.

Finally he turned, and Becky got a glimpse of his face for the first time. He looked like Tuck had hit him in the stomach with his football. Hard.

"What you need is a mother," Susannah said.

It was two mornings later, and they were walking up the road toward the gate where the school bus stopped. It was the first day of school, and, as a treat, Taggart had allowed her to spend the night with Susannah so they could walk to the bus together.

He seemed to remember that having a friend on the first day always helped, even if you'd been going to the same school your whole life. He was good about things like that, so Becky wanted things to be good for him, too.

But a *mother?* Becky looked at Susannah. "What for?"

"You *know* what for." Susannah gave her an impatient look and tossed her long dark hair. Susannah was a year older and she knew a lot. She rolled her eyes significantly.

"Oh," Becky said. "That."

Actually, she didn't know a lot about *that.* Not when it had to do with men and women, anyway.

She knew about bulls and cows. She'd seen artificial inseminations. It seemed like a good idea to her—less messy. She didn't know how her dad felt about it. She didn't think it was something she ought to ask.

"I'm not sure I want a mother."

"What's wrong with a mother?" Susannah sounded offended.

"I don't know. I haven't ever had one, have I? Well, not for long, anyway." Becky shifted her backpack from one shoulder to the other and scuffed the toes of her cowboy boots in the dirt.

"I guess not," Susannah said, contemplating Becky's mother's desertion. Then she said, "But you know mine. You like her, don't you?"

Becky nodded. Sometimes she envied Susannah her mother. It had been different when her grandmother was still around the house. But now that Grandma was in Bozeman, no one ever baked cookies or canned tomatoes or bought new barrettes for her hair.

Tess did all those things. She was also good with Band-Aids when you skinned your knee. Taggart believed in toughing it out—they didn't have a Band-Aid in their house. He wasn't much good at barrettes, either, though he could braid well enough.

It came from making bull ropes, he'd told her. Becky doubted if mothers learned to braid that way, but she didn't suppose it really mattered. And he did try.

"Well, then," Susannah went on, "you'll just have to get yours back."

Becky looked up, startled. "Get Julie back?"

"If that's her name. I got my dad, didn't I?"

"It's not the same. I mean, he didn't even know about you, so you can't blame him for not being there. But Julie knew... about me, I mean—" she said this last bit with difficulty, because it always made her feel funny somewhere in the middle of her stomach "—and she left, anyway."

Susannah kicked a rock. "She was a jerk."

Becky thought so, too, but she felt obligated to say what her father had always told her. "She just couldn't handle things. Daddy says she didn't know what she was getting into marrying him. The rodeos and the ranch and all. She was from New York City."

"That's no excuse."

"No." Becky agreed with that. "Well, you can see why I don't want her—if I've got to find a mother, I mean." She kicked the rock Susannah had kicked. They followed it up the road, taking turns.

"Then we'll find you another one."

"I'm not having Kitzy Miller!" Kitzy Miller worked in the Minimart. She chewed gum a pack at a time, had zits but called them freckles, and practically drooled on Taggart's boots whenever they stopped to buy gas or milk or bread.

There was no doubt in Becky's mind that Kitzy Miller had her eye on Taggart—and no way on earth was she going to have Kitzy for a mother!

"Definitely not Kitzy Miller," Susannah agreed fervently.

"Then who?"

They looked at each other hopefully, but neither could come up with another name. There were not a lot of unattached women in Elmer, Montana.

Becky kicked the rock. "Miss Setsma's nice."

"Miss Setsma's old as your grandma!" Susannah said about their piano teacher. She gave the rock an extrahard kick. "What about Brenna Jamison? She's young—and she's pretty."

Brenna lived up the valley on the biggest ranch around— when she was home, which wasn't often. Mostly she was somewhere else doing art. She was a very famous painter, and she only came home when her daddy, old Otis Jamison, required what Taggart called a command performance. There didn't seem to be very many of them.

"I don't think so," Becky said. "I mean, she's nice . . . but I don't think she wants to stay around here."

They'd reached the gate where the bus stopped, and they slid between the posts without undoing the wire that held it fast. The bus was just coming over the rise.

"Tuck might know somebody," Susannah suggested.

"I know everybody Tuck knows," Becky said glumly. Tuck had been her best friend before Susannah came. Now he was nine and couldn't always be bothered with her. "There's no one."

"Then we'll pray."

Becky's eyes widened. "Pray?"

"Why not?" Susannah said as the bus stopped and they climbed on. "It worked for me."

Probably because Susannah was a lot better person than she was, Becky thought, slumping in her seat. The bus started up again and Becky stared out the window as it rumbled its way toward town. Susannah probably never climbed trees her daddy told her not to, and she always studied her spelling words, and it was even possible that she ate all her carrots. Becky hated carrots.

Would a mother make her eat carrots?

Maybe she could pray for one who would not. That might be worth a shot. As the bus trundled on, she screwed her eyes up tight and sent a prayer winging heavenward. The bus wound up the hill and down, then up another and down. It stopped. Becky kept praying, unsure how long she was supposed to keep it up. The bus began its journey once more.

"You got a pain or somethin'?"

Becky's eyes popped open. A red-haired, freckle-faced boy was standing in the aisle, staring at her. "Oh, hi, Tuck. I'm prayin'."

He looked dubious. "You? For what?"

Becky hesitated, unsure if she was supposed to tell or not. Was it like a wish that didn't come true unless you kept it a secret? She turned to ask Susannah, but she was leaning over the seat in front, talking to that snotty Lizbeth Caldwell. Becky certainly wasn't going to betray her ignorance in front of Lizbeth!

"I'll tell you later," she promised, partly for fear of jinxing a prayer she had no very great hopes for anyway, and partly because she knew Tuck would think she was out of her mind if she told him.

"A stepmother? You're prayin' for a stepmother?" he'd say. "Like Cinderella's?"

No way. She didn't want that! She wasn't sure what she wanted—besides no carrots. She tried to think about it. It would have to be someone who'd appeal to her dad, she guessed. Someone pretty who looked good in jeans would be a start. But then, she'd also have to be fun to have around. And she'd have to know about barrettes and Band-Aids, and it would be good if she could bake cookies and didn't care if kids got dirty sometimes or fell out of trees they weren't supposed to climb in the first place. They needed someone who'd love her and Taggart both.

A pretty tall order since her own mother obviously hadn't.

Becky thought it was asking an awful lot—even of God.

And then the bus stopped and she got off and walked into her class—and saw Ms. Albright standing there.

They were following her again.

When she stopped to stare at the display of nails, screwdrivers and wire cutters in Gilliam's Hardware, Felicity could see them reflected in the glass as they ducked behind the dusty Dodge pickup truck parked beside the curb. It was the third time this week she'd been tailed—by two little girls.

Becky Jones and Susannah Tanner.

Her students.

If she were still teaching in Southern California, Felicity might have understood. There, in the midst of the anonymous urban sprawl, stalking had sometimes seemed a way of life.

But *here*? In *Elmer, Montana?*

By a pair of third- and fourth-grade girls?

Felicity wondered if she was losing her mind. She didn't think so. In fact, for the first time in two years, she'd begun to think she'd finally recovered it.

Moving to Elmer had been the start. She had come last month when she inherited Uncle Fred's house. It was a completely unexpected windfall. She hadn't seen Uncle Fred since she was ten years old, when she and her mother had visited him for two weeks in the summer.

He'd been the eldest of her grandfather's brothers, the one with the wanderlust. He had traveled everywhere on the globe before finally settling in Elmer and taking over its small newspaper. When she came that summer, he'd let Felicity help him print it. She remembered being ink-smudged and totally happy. Those two weeks had been among Felicity's fondest memories.

They had apparently been among Uncle Fred's happiest, too, for in his will he left her his house and everything in it—lock, stock and printing press.

Felicity had been flabbergasted. And yet it had seemed like fate—a godsend—coming as it had, exactly two years to the day after her husband Dirk had been killed.

Dirk. Dear, wonderful Dirk. They'd only been married two-and-a-half years. Their lives, their hopes, their futures, were ahead of them as they waited for Dirk to finish school.

A graduate student in music, Dirk Albright had been a talented cellist—a gifted musician, but an even more gifted teacher. Everyone knew it—especially Felicity. She and Dirk had grown up together, they'd gone to high school and university back in Iowa together. When Dirk won a graduate fellowship at UCLA, they'd married and moved to California together.

"I don't want to go without you," he'd said to her. "Please come."

And over her family's objections, she had. She'd never considered doing anything else because she'd loved Dirk as desperately as he loved her.

They'd lived on a shoestring budget in a tiny apartment above a garage in Westwood. They ate macaroni and cheese, ramen noodles and peanut butter sandwiches seven nights a week, and thought they were the luckiest people on earth. Felicity drove an hour and fifteen minutes each way to the school where she taught. But Dirk could ride his bike to the university. What little they could save, they put toward the house they'd buy someday wherever Dirk got a college teaching job. They had plans, hundreds of them. They talked about them every night.

And then one afternoon after school Felicity had looked up to see a policeman standing in the door to her classroom. Gently, quietly, he told her that Dirk was dead.

Riding his bike home from class as he did every day, he'd been hit by a car.

"He never knew," the policeman assured her. "He didn't suffer."

Felicity did. For the past two years she had mourned her lost husband, her lost hopes, her lost dreams. Everything she'd hoped to be had depended on her life with Dirk. In the space of a single moment, she'd lost it all.

"Come home," her parents urged her. "Come back to Iowa."

But she couldn't. There were too many memories there. Everywhere she turned she would come face-to-face with the past she and Dirk had shared. "No," she told them. "I'll stay here. I have my job. I love the kids. I'll survive."

She did. She got through the next school year by submerging herself in her work, letting it consume her. If she didn't stop, she didn't have to think, to plan, to face life more than a day at a time. That was enough.

Then, a little more than a year after Dirk's death, her friend, Lori, said, "Listen, Felicity... I have a friend I'd like you to meet."

A man, she meant.

Felicity knew Lori meant well, but she wasn't interested. She didn't want to know that his name was Craig, that he was an aeronautical engineer who lived in the same apartment complex as Lori, that he liked music and surfing and playing basketball. "I can't," she said.

"So, maybe he's not the right one," Lori said philosophically. "I know another guy, a friend of my brother's."

But Felicity wasn't interested in him, either. There were other men over the next few months—men Lori found for her, men her brother Tom and her sister Cassandra told to drop by and see her while they were in L.A. There were even some men who found her without any help at all. Nice men, all of them.

But not Dirk.

"You can't mourn him forever," Lori told her. "He wouldn't want you to stop living, you know."

Yes, Felicity knew. Intellectually she nodded her head and agreed, but she couldn't make herself show any interest in men. The very thought of dating again left her numb, as if her feelings were encased in ice.

"There are a million eligible men in Southern California," Lori had told her impatiently one night. "There must be one who's right for you."

But if there was, Felicity didn't care. She had no desire to look for him. And she wished everyone else would stop looking, too.

But they didn't. So, when news of Uncle Fred's legacy dropped into her mailbox like the proverbial roast duck and Felicity remembered those few carefree days of childhood joy, the memory translated itself into a desire to go back once again.

Why not, after all? She had nothing to keep her here.

"You're going *where*?" Lori demanded.

"Elmer, Montana."

"You'll be back," Lori predicted.

But once she'd arrived, Felicity's chest expanded, her breathing deepened. She felt, as she looked around at the tiny higgledy-piggledy town, the high mountains and the big, big sky, as if that first deep breath had finally cracked the ice. The pain and numbness she'd lived with since Dirk's death began almost imperceptibly to melt away.

Felicity had looked around the town and smiled at its prosaic name. Nestled against the foothills of the Bridgers, looking across the fertile Shields Valley toward the mysterious Crazy Mountains, Elmer had, to Felicity's way of thinking, been misnamed. It should have been called Eden—or Paradise.

She decided to stay.

"You haven't seen it in the winter," Polly McMaster, who ran the post office, said.

But Felicity was looking forward to winter. The sameness of Southern California's seasons was one of the things she had never got used to. "I grew up in Des Moines. I can hardly wait."

Polly had looked skeptical, but Felicity knew it was true. And she felt alive here for the first time in two years. She went back to California just long enough to resign from her job and pack her things.

"You're kidding," Lori said.

Felicity shook her head and kept packing.

Lori watched, then sighed philosophically. "Well, fine. Maybe you'll meet a cowboy."

Felicity looked at her askance. "A cowboy?"

"This is Montana, isn't it?"

But Felicity hadn't met a cowboy yet. She had met most of Elmer's 217 inhabitants, though. Their sympathies had been immediately engaged by the pretty young widow Fred Morrison had left his house to, and they thought she was a right smart lady when she preferred Elmer to Southern California. It wasn't long before Maudie Gilliam, whose husband ran the hardware store, was bringing her gooseberry pies and Howie Ward was fixing her window screen and two old schoolteachers called Cloris and Alice were inviting her out for meat loaf at the Busy Bee, and old Mr. Eberhardt stumped over every afternoon with yesterday's Bozeman *Chronicle* so she'd have a big-city newspaper to read.

"Fred always liked to keep up," he told her.

"So will I," Felicity had assured him. She could read the want ads, she thought, and look for a job.

Serendipitously, a job found her.

Polly's sister, who had been the third- and fourth-grade teacher in Elmer's seventy-six-student school, discovered in mid-August that the long-hoped-for baby she was expecting was actually going to be triplets.

"She has to take it easy," Polly had told Felicity. "Stay flat on her back. And the babies aren't due until January."

So Felicity had a job.

And—for some unknown reason—two little girls tailing her.

She stopped as usual in the post office to pick up her mail. When she came out they were still there, one dark head and one light brown, peeping over the hood of a pickup. Felicity smothered a smile and turned up Apple Street, heading home.

Two small girls ducked and bobbed along behind.

They only came halfway down the block, just far enough to be sure that she was going into her house. When Felicity peeked out again moments later, they were gone. "What are you two up to?" she murmured as she let the curtain fall.

At first she had thought they had questions they were too shy to ask in class. Now she knew better. Susannah, a fourth grader, never seemed to have questions about anything, and every piece of work she turned in was excellent. Becky was a different story.

Not shy at all, Becky had all sorts of questions. Work was another matter. A third grader with bright green eyes and a quicksilver smile, Becky Jones had done absolutely nothing in three weeks.

Nothing—except wear spurs every day to school.

"They missed the bus *again?*" Taggart scowled when Noah put the cellular phone in the truck and ambled back to the corral to report the conversation he'd just had with his daughter. "How many times this week is that?"

Noah shook his head and began once more to slap paint on the fence. "Three. And three last week. You reckon Orville is takin' off the minute the bell rings?"

"Naw. He's been driving that bus since I was on it. It's gotta be that new teacher of theirs. She must be keeping 'em after."

"Susannah never does anything to get kept after school!"

"Takes after her mother, does she?" Taggart grinned. "Well, she will if she hangs around with Becky long enough."

It wasn't that his daughter was a bad kid; she was just a challenging one. He figured it must run in the family. His dad had always said Taggart made life "interesting" for his parents. He supposed it was only fair that Becky made life interesting for him.

"So, who goes and gets 'em today?" Noah asked.

"Oughta make 'em walk," Taggart grumbled, but he set down his brush and started toward the truck. "I'll go."

Noah grinned. "Want to get a look at the teacher, do you?"

Taggart stopped. "No, why?"

Noah shoved his hat back. "Susannah says she's a looker. Long blond hair, deep blue eyes. Didn't Becky tell you?"

"Becky wouldn't notice."

If it didn't have four legs—or eight—his daughter didn't know it was there. Becky noticed frogs and spiders and mice. She played with cats and puppies and colts. She didn't pay the least bit of attention to people—unless they were riding on horses. Or bulls.

He doubted if she even knew her new teacher's name. And it would certainly never occur to her to tell him the woman was pretty.

Not that he'd be interested if she did.

Taggart Jones might have a wistful hormonal twinge every now and then—hell, what thirty-two-year-old man in possession of all the right hormones didn't?—but he could handle them.

Far better than he could handle another marriage.

So what if Noah and Tess were disgustingly happy in theirs? So what if both Noah's brothers, Tanner and Luke, and Taggart's friend, Mace—all well married—were as pleased as pigs in mud? That didn't mean he would be, even if he found someone he was ga-ga over.

Which he hadn't. Wouldn't. Because, damn it, he wasn't looking.

Oh, maybe he allowed his eyes to follow a pair of long legs and a curvy bottom in a pair of tight jeans from time to time. And maybe he wondered sometimes what it would be like these days to kiss a girl over the age of eight. But those were his hormones talking, not his common sense.

Taggart's common sense told him that he'd had his shot with a woman and he'd blown it—big-time. It had taken him less than a year to drive Julie away. He didn't imagine another woman would want to hang around any longer than she had, even though he wasn't going down the road all year long anymore.

He had other drawbacks now—like an almost eight-year-old girl.

Not that he personally considered Becky a drawback. As far as he was concerned, his daughter was the best thing that had ever happened to him.

He might not think too highly of Julie in other respects, but he thanked God every day for the daughter she'd given him.

And since she'd hated him and their life so much, he even thanked God that she'd left. He did it again now as he started up the truck and headed toward town.

He and Becky were doing fine just the way they were.

Two

"May I please speak to Mr. or Mrs. Jones?"

Accustomed to calls from cowboys wanting to sign up for bull- and bronc-riding school or livestock dealers intent on selling him or his dad some cattle, Taggart was startled when the voice he heard was female, soft in his ear, yet clear and warm like honey. His folks must be making new friends.

He leaned against the barn door and tucked the cellular phone against his shoulder. "Sorry. They've moved to Bozeman."

"Bozeman?" The woman sounded flustered. "But I thought... This is Felicity Albright. I teach their daughter, Becky...."

Taggart fumbled the phone. Hell, how was he supposed to know she wanted him? Nobody ever called him Mr. Jones! And everybody knew there wasn't a Mrs. Jones, didn't they? He'd forgotten that Becky's teacher was new in town.

He rescued the phone and cleared his throat. "Sorry. I thought you meant... never mind. I'm Becky's dad."

"Ah." He could hear relief in her voice. "I'm so glad to

reach you, Mr. Jones. I'd like to talk with you. I wondered if you could drop by some afternoon?''

"Talk with me? Like a conference, you mean? I thought conferences were in October."

"Well, yes. I realize it's a little early, but—'' she hesitated "—there are some things I'd like to discuss with you.''

Like why she was making Becky miss the bus every night? That'd be nice, Taggart thought. He straightened, shrugging his shoulders against the wooden door. "I wouldn't mind discussin' a few things with you, either, Ms., um—'' What the hell had she said her name was?

"Albright," she supplied in his groping silence. "I gather Becky hasn't been talking much about school?''

"I reckon she's got other things on her mind.''

"I reckon.'' Her echo of his words seemed somewhat dry. "That's one of the things I'd like to discuss with you, Mr. Jones. When can you come?''

"Tomorrow?'' Might as well get it over with. Maybe she'd stop keeping Becky after school that way, too.

"Wonderful. About three-fifteen or so?''

"Why not? I been coming in three times a week anyhow. You know they been missing the bus, don't you?'' He knew he sounded accusing, but he had a right to. She'd been inconveniencing everybody. He'd intended to tell her yesterday when he picked the girls up, but she hadn't been anywhere around.

"I thought they must be.''

"And you kept 'em, anyhow?''

"I haven't been keeping them, Mr. Jones. Becky and Susannah are choosing to stay late.''

His brows hiked up. He'd always known his daughter was bright and clever and capable, but he'd never known her to expend much of that brilliance or cleverness on school before. "How come?''

"I was hoping you could tell me.''

"What do you mean?''

"Perhaps it would be better if we discussed it tomorrow. I do want you to know, though, how much I've been enjoying Becky in class. She's very...interesting. A challenge.''

That sounded ominous. But then, maybe this Ms. Albright was one of those rigid, toe-the-line types who didn't appreciate a little girl who marched to a different drummer. Taggart rubbed his back against the barn door again and vowed to stick up for Becky. "She's a good kid," he said defensively.

"Yes, she is. I'm looking forward to meeting you, Mr. Jones."

"I'll be there."

Felicity felt a little foolish asking for a conference with Becky's parents. It wasn't as if the little girl was doing anything dreadful. She wasn't.

She wasn't doing anything at all. No work. No papers. Nothing.

Except wearing spurs. And tailing her teacher after school. And on Saturday, too, now—if last Saturday was anything to go by.

Felicity had been standing in the checkout line at the grocery store when she glanced up and saw Becky and Susannah peeping in the window. The moment they realized she'd seen them, they ran off.

Felicity had been tempted to ask Carol Ferguson, the checker, if she'd ever been tailed around town. Was it perhaps something all newcomers to Elmer experienced? But somehow the topic never came up—and it wasn't easily worked into a conversation. But eventually Felicity expected she'd get to the bottom of it. Maybe when she met the Joneses.

She had to admit to a certain curiosity about Becky's parents. Her father, according to Becky, was a bull rider. A world champion bull rider.

"He rode nine out of ten bulls at the National Finals two years ago. And I'm gonna be just like him when I grow up." She never mentioned her mother. Obviously the father had all the charisma in the family.

Felicity supposed his wife was one of those long-suffering women who stood by their men or, in this case, stood waiting for them to come home, which might not seem very romantic to a child, but certainly, to Felicity's way of thinking, wasn't to be scoffed at.

She knew very little about rodeo herself. She'd never met a bull rider. A third-grade teacher who'd been married to a concert cellist didn't travel in the same circles with professional bull riders. It seemed a pretty exotic thing to be. She was amazed that you could make a living at it. She doubted very many people could. But apparently until two years ago, Becky's father had. Now, according to Becky, he was staying home.

"Teaching," Becky had announced just last week. "Like you."

"I thought you said he was a bull rider."

"He was. Is. Now he teaches. How to ride bulls."

Felicity couldn't imagine. Did he give tests? Homework? Draw up lesson plans?

She'd have to ask him, she thought with a smile as she sat at her desk and graded a math quiz. The Joneses would be here any moment. Without their daughter. Becky and Susannah had made it onto the bus this afternoon. Felicity had stood right next to it until it pulled away just to make sure. Not that they seemed to have any desire to linger.

Becky had, in fact, been bouncing with suppressed excitement all afternoon. Felicity wondered at it, but could hardly ask. Did she know her parents were coming to meet her teacher? Was she pleased?

It didn't seem likely—not since all Becky had to show for the first three weeks of school was a string of zeroes in the grade book after her name.

The sound of footsteps at the doorway made her look up, smiling in the expectation of seeing Becky's parents.

She saw the handsomest cowboy she'd ever seen.

Lean and tanned, broad-shouldered and narrow-hipped, he was the epitome of every woman's western fantasy. Lori, she thought irrelevantly, would have approved.

His hat was a Stetson, his jeans were Wranglers, and his dusty boots looked like they had been places that would turn an urban cowboy pale. He was not, she noted, wearing spurs. Obviously, then, he was not Mr. Jones.

Her perusal took far longer than it should have. When she recollected herself, she realized he'd been making an equally astonished study of her. She reddened. "May I help you?" she said coolly, trying to regain her equilibrium.

He reached up and jerked off his Stetson, baring a short thatch of thick dark hair. "I'm . . . looking for Ms. Albright?" He clearly thought he hadn't found her.

Felicity wiped suddenly damp palms on her jungle-print skirt and stood up, holding out her hand as she came around the desk. "I'm Felicity Albright."

"Taggart Jones." He took her hand.

"I...I'm so glad you could come, Mr. Jones," Felicity said, her mouth oddly dry.

"Taggart," he corrected her. "If you call me Mr. Jones, I'll be lookin' over my shoulder for my dad." The grin he flashed her must have sent women all over the rodeo circuit into a tail-spin.

Felicity, who had been immune to that sort of thing from anyone other than Dirk, felt a faint stirring deep within. It surprised her so much that she jerked her hand out of his grasp.

He didn't seem sorry to break the contact. He quickly stuffed his hand into the pocket of his jeans. The other tightened on the brim of his hat. "Pleased to meet you, ma'am." He dipped his head, and for an instant, his gaze trapped hers. He had the most intensely green eyes she had ever seen. Deep-set and sparkling, they reminded her of a pool in a forest glen, a pattern of sunlight and shadow on a jade both still and deep.

How fanciful is that, she chided herself, disgusted. She didn't ordinarily wax poetic about the parents of the children she taught. "I'm delighted to meet you, too, Mr., er...Taggart. Won't you sit down?" She gestured toward one of the children's chairs. "Becky has talked a lot about you."

"She has?" He sounded doubtful. He tried to sit in one of the children's chairs, then another. Both were far too small, and after trying for several seconds to find a comfortable spot, he gave up and swung himself up to sit on the waist-high counter above her storage cupboard, his boots dangling.

"Sorry," he apologized, but his grin was as unrepentant as Becky's. "I used to get into trouble for sittin' up here when I was in school. You gonna make me get down, too?"

Felicity tried to resist his grin. "I'd have to," she told him in her best severe-schoolmarm voice, "if the children were here. Since they aren't—" she shrugged and smiled, her tone softening "—no, I won't."

Their gazes caught again. Something electric seemed to hover in the air. Abruptly, Felicity looked away and slipped behind her desk, grateful for the solid expanse of wood that separated her from Taggart Jones.

What was the matter with her? He was Becky's father! He was *married!*

It was just that dratted Lori and her subliminal suggestion about a cowboy, Felicity told herself—and the sudden reactivation of her two-years-asleep hormones. She drew a steadying breath and pulled out her grade book. "I'm sorry Mrs. Jones couldn't make it."

"There isn't one."

The baldness of his statement rocked her. His tone was matter-of-fact, but embarrassment burned her cheeks, anyway. Why hadn't she checked? When half her California students had been from single-parent families, why had she assumed that none of her Montana kids would be?

"I'm sorry," she said.

He shrugged. "Not your fault. She left us when Becky was two months old. It's common knowledge hereabouts. I should've said when you asked for her, but that was when I thought you were asking for my mom. And then when you weren't, I guess I was more concerned about Becky."

Felicity felt like a fool. She twisted her pencil and finally mustered a smile. But when Taggart smiled back, and all those dormant hormones suddenly took it upon themselves to dance around again, she looked down at her grade book. "Er, yes, well, um…Becky. She's quite a…an interesting child. She told me she wants to be a bull rider like her father."

Taggart rubbed a hand against the back of his neck. "It's what she knows. She'll figure out sooner or later that there's plenty better ways to make a living."

"She's very proud of you."

"I'm proud of her, too." Their gazes met again. This time Felicity kept her hormones under strict control.

"Of course you are," she said, and wondered how she could gracefully ease into the part of the conference that he might not be so proud of.

"So, what's wrong with her?" he said, neatly solving her dilemma.

"Wrong?"

He grinned. "Nobody ever called my folks to talk about me when I was doin' everything I was supposed to. You got a problem with Becky, I want to hear it."

Felicity sucked in her breath. "You're absolutely right. There are one or two things I hope you can help me with." She opened her grade book. "As you can see—" she turned the book so he could follow the line of zeroes her finger traced "—Becky hasn't turned any work in all year. Now, there may have been some things she wasn't quite sure about, but I'm certain she can—"

"Hasn't turned anything in? *Nothing?* All year?" Taggart's grin vanished. He bounded down off the counter and came to loom over her.

"There have been several reading work sheets due already, as you can see. Not large assignments, of course. But she hasn't done any of them. And here—" she turned the page "—is a record of the arithmetic assignments I've given them." More zeroes. "We've finished our first unit in social studies." Still another line of zeroes. She showed him the incomplete for the science project, the penmanship grade— "Not really important," she allowed. "But another indication . . ."

Taggart's jaw tightened. The deep tan on his face was underlined by an even deeper red beneath. He scowled fiercely. "Becky always does her work! She never misses." Felicity didn't know whether he was talking to her or to himself.

"In the past, you mean? Then . . . there isn't any reason, um, at home . . . why she might not be . . ."

"A reason at home for her not doing her work? Hell, no. But I'll give her a damn good one for doing it!"

"I'm sure you will." Felicity felt a flicker of sympathy for Becky Jones. "But I'd really like to know *why* she isn't doing any now—especially if you say she's always done her work before."

Taggart shook his head. He walked across the room and stared at the children's stories she'd hung on the wall, scowling at them. "Susannah doin' hers?"

"Yes, all of it. And very well, too."

He raked a hand through his hair, ruffling it where his hat had jammed it down. "I don't know, then. I figured maybe if Susannah wasn't doin' hers, either . . . They're friends, you see."

"I know. They...do a lot together. That's another thing I wanted to talk to you about." She hesitated, unsure how to phrase it.

Taggart leaned against the counter, arms folded across his chest. Felicity had to look up to meet his gaze. If she didn't, her eyes were on a level with his big gold world championship belt buckle. She studied it. Her eyes lowered a bit farther. Bad idea.

"What else?" he demanded.

There was only the bald truth. "Becky and Susannah seem to be...following me."

"Following you?" He gaped at her.

"You said they were missing the bus," she reminded him quickly. "Some days after school when I'm walking home or to the grocery store or wherever I'm going, I look back and they're...following me."

Taggart frowned again, but it wasn't so much a frown of anger now as one of total bafflement. "This is a small town. You could just happen to look around and see them."

"I know it's a small town. That's how I know they're following me. You notice things like that. *I* notice things like that. And whenever I glance over my shoulder—at the library, at the Laundromat, at the grocery store—there they are."

"An' you think they're doing it deliberately?"

"I would say so, yes. It's happened several times a week since the beginning of school. I thought you might have some idea..."

"Not a clue. She's never done anything like it before. Of course, she's never not done her work before, either. Damn." Taggart scratched the back of his head. He slapped his hat against his thigh and shoved away from the counter. "I'll sort her out. I'll get to the bottom of it, Ms. Albright. Believe me." He started toward the door.

Felicity went after him. "Uh, Mr. Jones? Taggart?"

He turned. "There's more?"

"One...other thing."

He waited, not speaking.

"Spurs."

"What?"

Felicity shrugged helplessly. "She's wearing...spurs."

He stared. *"To school?"*

Felicity nodded. "Every day. Except the first day. I don't remember her wearing them then. But it was pretty chaotic. Still," she mused, "I think I would have noticed."

"I'd bet on it," Taggart said darkly. He smacked one fist into his other palm. "When I get my hands on that kid—"

"There isn't really a rule about it," Felicity said quickly. "I checked."

"Don't reckon anybody ever figured you'd need one." Taggart strangled his hat brim. "Spurs! Damn that kid. What's she up to?"

"Perhaps she wants attention."

"She'll get it, believe me."

"I didn't ask you to come in so I'd get her in trouble," she said quickly. "I simply wanted to understand what was going on."

"You and me both." He fixed his gaze on her. "Did you ask her?" he said. "About the spurs?"

"She said she needed to wear them."

"*Needed to?*" Taggart's eyes narrowed. He frowned, and the line between his dark brows deepened. "And what about the following business? Did you ask her about that?"

"I didn't want to accuse them of something." Felicity gave a little shrug. "I mean, I'm not from Elmer and I didn't want to... get off on the wrong foot. I thought it was maybe some local custom...."

"Not one I ever heard of." Taggart started toward the door again, then turned back once more. "Is that all?"

"That's all." She ventured a smile.

He didn't return it. "It's enough." He drew himself up straighter and squared his shoulders. "I appreciate your calling me, ma'am. I'll take care of it. And there'll be lots of work and no more following you around, I promise."

"Thank you." Felicity gave him a grateful smile. "And the spurs?"

"No more spurs." Taggart set his hat on his head and tugged it down tight. "Count on it."

He didn't know whether he was madder at Becky or at himself. He was plenty annoyed at his daughter, that was for sure.

And puzzled, too. But he'd sort her out pronto, no two ways about it. He only wished he could sort himself out as quick.

That was Becky's teacher? That young knockout of a blonde? They sure as hell hadn't made teachers like her when he was a kid!

"A looker," Noah had called her. The word didn't begin to describe Felicity Albright. When he'd first glanced at her sitting there behind the teacher's desk, Taggart had thought she was some high school girl who came to help out. But then he'd taken a closer look and realized she was old enough to teach. She was just too damn pretty!

And all his wistful hormones sure as hell noticed. He couldn't remember being knocked for a loop like that since Julie. And the simple memory of that had nearly sent him running.

She wasn't Julie, he reminded himself. She was a teacher. His kid's teacher. And he'd been there to talk to her—like the concerned, intelligent, mature parent he was.

Still, he was lucky he'd managed to cross the room without stumbling over his boots. Remembering the way he'd stared and his initial stammering awkwardness, Taggart cursed under his breath now as he drove up the highway toward the ranch. The beautiful Ms. Albright must think he was an idiot.

And that he had an idiot for a kid.

Damn Becky, anyway! What on earth was she doing? How could she not turn in any work for three full weeks? How could she tail her teacher after school? And for God's sake, what was with the spurs? *Spurs!*

Taggart's fingers tightened on the steering wheel. Was she upset because his folks had moved away? Was she trying to say she'd be happier if he let her go live with them in Bozeman?

His mother had offered to let her come with them, though she knew Taggart would never agree. When he left rodeoing after the accident, he'd done it because he wanted to be with Becky. He still wanted it.

Didn't she?

Maybe not. Maybe...oh, hell, there were a million maybes. Most of the time his daughter was an open book. Not for her the feminine wiles that so entranced and then entangled him with Julie! She wasn't ever going to be like her mother, he assured himself time and again.

Now he wondered if he knew her at all.

As he pulled into the yard at Noah's new house, he saw Becky's sun-streaked hair and Susannah's dark head in the window of the tree house he and Noah had built for them. They peered down at him as he shut the engine off, but the moment he opened the door, both heads abruptly disappeared.

He stalked over to the tree. "Rebecca Kathleen! Get your rear end down here!"

There was a mouselike scuffling overhead, then Becky's green eyes appeared in the window. "Oh, hi, Daddy."

Hands on hips, he glowered up at her. "Down. Now."

"But we were just—"

"Down, Rebecca."

Her head disappeared again.

"That's twice he's called you Rebecca," he heard Susannah whisper. "You'd better go."

"I'm goin'." Becky didn't sound nearly as nervous as she ought to. Taggart tapped the toe of his boot on the dirt.

"Taggart!" He turned to see Tess, with Clay balanced on one hip, waving at him from the kitchen door. "Have time for a glass of lemonade?"

"Not today. Thanks, anyway. Just collectin' my kid."

When he turned back, Becky was climbing down the ladder. She was wearing dusty blue jeans, a T-shirt. And spurs. Taggart's teeth came together with a snap.

"I gotta get my backpack," Becky said the instant her feet hit the ground. She skirted around him quickly, heading toward the house.

"Got a lot of homework, have you?"

Becky looked back at him guiltily, gave a tiny nod, then scurried toward the house. She seemed, for the first time, just a little nervous.

She damned well ought to be. Taggart went back to the truck and leaned against the door, arms folded across his chest. Out of the corner of his eye he could see Susannah peeking down at him from the window of the tree house. Usually she came skipping right up to him, ready to share some bit of news. Not today.

Becky retrieved her backpack, answered something Tess had said, then trudged toward him across the yard. There was a definite reluctance in her walk now. She didn't look at him, just climbed into the passenger side of the truck and fastened her seat belt without him even having to remind her.

Taggart got in, flicked on the engine, threw the truck into reverse and backed around. Becky sat silently beside him. Every now and then she slanted him a quick glance, like someone checking the fuse on a stick of dynamite she'd set.

The entire ride was accomplished in silence. She didn't even ask to steer the truck through the gate while he opened and closed it. Taggart didn't remark on it. They reached the kitchen before either of them said a word.

Becky headed for the stairs. "I gotta go do my homework."

"Why start now?"

She flinched as if she'd been shot. Then she ventured a wary look at him over her shoulder. He beckoned to her. Sighing, she turned and came to stand in front of him, looking up at him solemnly, like a condemned prisoner about to face the firing squad. Taggart felt a momentary remorse, then promptly squelched it. She was in the wrong, not him.

"So," he said evenly, "why don't you tell me what's going on?"

Becky blinked. Her eyes widened fractionally. "Going on?"

"You know I went to see your teacher today."

She nodded.

"And you must have a pretty good idea what she told me."

Another nod, this one a little more hesitant.

"Want to guess what she told me?"

"Um…" She paused and ran her tongue over her lips. "That I didn't do my homework?"

"Homework, hell! You haven't done *any* work! Not a lick. Not since school started!" His eyes narrowed when she nodded again. "You're *agreeing* with me?"

She swallowed audibly, then straightened her shoulders and looked at him steadily. "Yes."

"She also told me you're wearing spurs to school."

Becky pressed her lips together. Something flickered in her gaze and was quickly suppressed. She shifted her feet. The spurs jingled. "Uh-huh."

Taggart felt a muscle in his jaw tick. "And she said you're following her all over town!"

Becky looked at him, horrified. *"She saw us?"* Then she sighed and stuffed her hands into the pockets of her jeans. Once more impassiveness covered her features. Her green gaze met his unflinchingly.

"So maybe you'd like to tell me why?"

Becky dug the toe of her cowboy boot into the linoleum floor, contemplating it for a moment before she lifted her gaze. "So she'd notice me."

"Oh, she did that," Taggart said dryly. "At the Laundromat. At the grocery store—"

"Not the followin'," Becky amended. "We didn't want her to notice *that.* Just the other stuff."

He shook his head, uncomprehending. "Why?"

"So she'd call you."

Which left him no more enlightened than before. He scratched his head. "You wanted her to call me?"

"Uh-huh."

He stared at her as if he might find the answer to his unspoken question emblazoned on her forehead, but he didn't. So eventually he had to ask again. "Why?"

"So you could meet her before some other guy did."

"What?"

Becky shrugged guilelessly. "She's better'n that lady at the rodeo in Missoula. Heaps better. Better'n Kitzy Miller, too."

Taggart took a step back and gripped the doorjamb for support. "Better than *what* lady in Missoula? What's this about Kitzy Miller?"

He knew he was perilously close to shouting at her. All right, he *was* shouting at her, but she wasn't making any sense! He swallowed hard and looked at her closely. "Explain."

Becky hunched her shoulders. "Well, I know she's not Tess, but she's the next best thing and—"

"Whoa. Hang on here a minute, sweetheart. What's this about Tess?" He hesitated, a notion suddenly occurring to him. He crossed the room and hunkered down to get on eye level with his daughter. He settled his big hands on her narrow shoulders. "Is this about mothers, Pard?"

She shifted under his hands. "Sorta." She wouldn't meet his eyes.

The vague worry that sometimes bothered him in the dark of night began to creep up on him in the bright light of day—the worry that said he wasn't a good enough parent, that he'd failed Becky as well as having failed her mother.

He made himself ask, "Do you want a mother?"

Her toe scraped. A spur jingled. "Not exac'ly," she said at last. "But if I'm gonna get one," she added firmly, "I'd rather have Miz Albright than Kitzy Miller or that lady at the rodeo."

Taggart stared at her, astonished. "What makes you think you're going to get any of them?"

"The way you look at 'em."

Taggart felt a flush crawl up his neck. He stood abruptly and tugged at the collar of his shirt. "How do I look at them?" he asked, then wasn't sure he wanted to know.

"Like you want 'em," Becky said bluntly. "The way I looked at dogs before I got Digger."

Taggart rubbed a hand down his face. "God," he muttered. He wasn't sure if it was supplication or blasphemy—probably the former. Heaven knew he needed all the help he could get. He looked like he wanted a woman? *That* was why his daughter hadn't been doing her schoolwork? *That* was why she and Susannah had been following Felicity Albright around town? *That* was why she was wearing spurs to school? So he could meet her teacher and—

And what?

Bed Felicity Albright? He didn't think that would have occurred to Becky.

Then what?

Marry her?

Taggart groaned and closed his eyes.

Three

───

He tried gentleness; he tried firmness; he tried logic; he tried emotion. Basically, he ranted and raved about how finding a woman was his responsibility, not hers, *if* he wanted a woman, which he didn't. Did she understand? He glowered. He glared. He stomped from one end of the room to the other and back.

Through it all Becky sat against the back of the couch, hands folded in her lap, moving only to point the toes of her boots in and out, in and out, as she watched him pace.

"It's not that I don't appreciate your...efforts," Taggart finished finally. "I know you...mean well. But—" here he stopped and fixed her with a steely look "—it's wrong to meddle in other people's lives. And you have to admit that not doing any work was pretty ill-advised."

For the first time Becky's lower lip jutted and began to quiver just a little. He took heart, glad he was beginning to get through to her.

Determined, he pressed on. "And so was wearing those da—dratted spurs." He gave her a hard look. "There will be no more spurs in school. Got that?"

Becky nodded once. She looked suitably chastened now. He almost hated to bring up the following Ms. Albright business, fearing it might be overkill, but he needed to make sure she got the point about that, too.

"And you will not follow your teacher anymore, either. Understand?"

A quick, flicking glance in his direction. "Yes, Daddy." Then she lowered her eyes again.

"Good." He gave a satisfied sigh, glad they had that straightened out, glad she realized she had no business meddling in his love life, glad there would be no more matchmaking.

Her head was bent. She was still studying her hands. Taggart, looking at her, was sure he felt worse than she did about her chastisement. Then she gave a tiny sniffle.

"Ah, hell, Pard," he muttered, undone, and strode over to grab her off the couch. She practically leapt into his arms, hugging him fiercely around the neck and wrapping her legs around his waist, kicking him in the butt with her spurs as she did so. He didn't care. He relished the strength of those small arms hugging him. He hugged her back and nuzzled her neck, making her squirm and giggle.

"I love you, Pard," he said at last, his throat tight.

She grinned and gave him a smacking kiss. "Love you, too, Daddy." She squirmed some more until he let her slide to the floor. Then she looked up at him, and they smiled at each other.

"I'll start dinner," he said. "You go get your schoolwork done." He picked up her backpack and handed it to her. She took it and started toward the stairs, then stopped and looked back at him.

"Miz Albright's awful pretty, isn't she, Daddy?"

"Becky!"

But he knew that his strangled exclamation and flushed face had given her the answer she was looking for.

"He likes her," Susannah said, looking up from the report she was writing on the history of the Shields Valley. It was part of the local history project that Ms. Albright had assigned, lots better than the boring stuff most teachers made them do. But today they had more important things on their minds.

"He thinks she's pretty," Becky corrected as she bent over her map. She was supposed to be making a flour-and-water version of the Crazies, but the flour wasn't cooperating. Neither was the water. There was a lot more of both on her hands than there was on the fiber board.

"Men are like that," Susannah replied knowledgeably. "It's a start."

"Huh." Tuck snorted. He was sitting at the desk next to Becky, drawing an Indian on horseback, one of a series of illustrations he was making to show the people who'd lived in the valley throughout history, and it took all his concentration. When Tuck drew, he never paid attention to anything else. Becky was surprised he'd even heard them talking.

"'S true," Susannah said. "It's how come my dad fell in love with my mom—at first."

Tuck stuck his tongue in the corner of his mouth and bent over his drawing. Becky tried to scrape some of the flour-and-water paste off her hands onto the map and make it look like a snow-capped peak. Her nose itched and she wanted to scratch it. She wiggled it. That didn't help.

"Scratch my nose," she said to Sam Bacon, the other member of their group. On Monday Ms. Albright had divided the class into groups of four and put them to work on projects.

"Multimedia events," she called them. Susannah, who had the neatest handwriting, was doing the report; Tuck, because he was by far the best artist, was drawing the people; Becky—because she was the messiest probably—was making the map; And Sam, who wasn't much good at reading and writing, but could do anything with his hands, was sanding the butt of the wooden rifle replica he was making. Now he scratched her nose for her, then went back to sanding.

"How's the Shields Valley crew?"

Becky looked up to see Jenny Nichols, the school's one teacher's aide, smiling at them. Becky had to remember to call her Mrs. Nichols during school days. Outside of school she was always just Jenny. Becky had known her as long as she could remember.

Jenny and her husband, Mace, lived on the old Galveston spread up past Flathead Creek. They'd finally saved enough to buy it just a year ago. Before that Mace had cowboyed for

Becky's grandpa and had run his small herd with Will Jones's bigger one. As soon as Becky was big enough to walk, she'd followed Mace.

"Shadow," he called her, and then he'd grin the most gorgeous grin Becky had ever seen and her heart would do a flip-flop. With his black hair and deep blue eyes and that wide white grin, Mace Nichols was the handsomest cowboy Becky had ever known.

And the nicest—next to her dad.

Sometimes she wished Mace wasn't already married to Jenny, because then he could wait and marry her. But she'd always liked Jenny, too. Once or twice she'd even thought it would be nice to have Jenny for a mom. If Jenny divorced Mace and married Becky's dad that would leave Mace free to someday marry her. She wondered if he'd like having his ex-wife for a mother-in-law.

Maybe it wasn't such a good idea, after all.

"Mace wants to know when you're coming out to visit us," Jenny said. Sometimes her dad let her go spend the weekend or a few days in the summer with Mace and Jenny, but she hadn't gone now since school had started. She'd been too busy trying to get her father together with Ms. Albright.

Now Becky shrugged. "I dunno. I've got a lot of work to do here."

Jenny grinned. "So I heard."

Becky flushed, realizing that Jenny knew about her three weeks of missing schoolwork. She hoped Mace didn't find out. He'd be disappointed in her.

He might approve if he understood why she was doing it, though, because he and Jenny were happy enough. But then again, maybe he wouldn't because he was a good friend of her dad's, and sometimes grown-ups stuck together.

"How about coming out this weekend for a while," Jenny suggested.

"Maybe." But Becky knew she couldn't. She and Susannah had to carry out the second phase of their plan.

"There's more?" Becky had said doubtfully when Susannah proposed it.

"He didn't propose to her the first time he saw her, did he?"

"Well, no," Becky had admitted. So they were moving on to phase two—as soon as Taggart had a week or so to calm down.

Becky slanted a quick glance at Ms. Albright. Did she think Taggart was handsome the way Becky thought Mace was handsome? Did he make her feel all hot and cold and kind of quivery inside?

Was that the way her dad made Kitzy Miller feel?

Becky didn't like to think about that. Her cheeks warmed suddenly when she realized that Ms. Albright had lifted her eyes from the paper she'd been reading and was looking straight at her. Becky ducked her head and shoved her hands in her pockets.

Only then did she realize they were still covered with paste.

She missed them.

Perverse as it might be, Felicity felt just a little bereft every afternoon when she left school and glanced over her shoulder to discover that "the shadow twins," as she'd come to think of them, weren't lurking there.

They weren't at the grocery store on Saturday morning. They weren't at the museum-cum-library Wednesday afternoon. They weren't outside the Laundromat on Tuesday when she carried her basket of folded laundry home. Every day after school they got on the bus like good little girls. Becky wasn't even wearing spurs.

It was just the way it should be.

And yet Felicity kept wondering what had caused Becky's behavior in the first place.

She'd hoped that Taggart—she really did think of him as Taggart even though she told herself she ought to be calling him Mr. Jones—might call and tell her. But three days went by, and then a week, and he never rang.

Even more perplexing was the new mystery she had to contemplate: why she spent so much time thinking about Taggart Jones?

If he'd been at all like Dirk, she might have understood it. But he wasn't. Dirk had been tall, three inches over six feet, with straight fair hair that, in the sun, turned to strands of spun gold. He'd had deep brown eyes all the more striking because they were at such odds with his pale coloring. He was quiet, introspective, a man in tune with music very few people heard.

Taggart Jones was average in height, his skin weathered and suntanned, his green eyes framed by lines drawn by laughter and the sun. His hair was short and dark, what she could see of it. Mostly it was hidden by his hat. His *cowboy* hat, she reminded herself.

Never in a million years had she anticipated being interested in a cowboy.

She wasn't really interested, she'd tried assuring herself. Her hormones had suddenly come back to life, and he'd happened to be around at the time.

It could have been any man.

If Elmer had more of a social life, she could have tested out her theory. But single men were not thick on the ground in Elmer, and so she spent more time than she wanted to recall fantasizing about Taggart Jones.

Not at school, of course. She never had time at school. But at night when she was sitting at home grading papers or cooking dinner or fooling around with Uncle Fred's old printing press, she'd find herself daydreaming about a dark-haired cowboy who wore a Stetson and boots and a big gold buckle and had eyes the color of a mountain glade.

It was just that there was nothing else to think about—besides school—she told herself. And school meant thinking about Becky, and thinking about Becky meant thinking about Taggart—and there she'd be, thinking about him again.

He had certainly been as good as his word.

Becky had appeared sans spurs the next morning, and she hadn't missed an assignment since. In fact, she had turned in every single assignment for the entire first three weeks!

"It's too late to get credit," Felicity had said.

"Don't matter." Becky thrust the papers at her. "My dad said to do 'em."

And she had. Very well. She'd understood everything, which told Felicity that lack of comprehension hadn't been the problem.

Then what was?

"My dad says to apologize to you, too. For the spurs. An' the work I didn't do." Becky flushed. "An' the following." She ducked her head briefly, then raised it again. Her eyes were mountain-glade green and as steady and direct as her father's.

"Apology accepted." Felicity smiled at her.

Becky smiled back. A hopeful smile? That's what it looked like to Felicity, but she didn't know and Becky didn't explain. She just took off running toward the playground.

Bemused, Felicity watched her go, still wishing she knew what had been going on. But short of calling Taggart and asking him, she didn't suppose she ever would. Still, she thought now, with an odd little hope of her own, Elmer was the small town he'd claimed it was. Maybe if she waited long enough, she'd run into him sometime.

He ran into her everywhere.

Of course, it was his fault. Every time he turned around now he seemed to have to go into town. Wednesday just before dinner, for example, Becky remembered the book she'd forgotten to get to do her report. So they'd had to drive into Elmer to the tiny museum-cum-library to pick it up. And coincidentally the woman standing talking to the museum volunteer was none other than Felicity Albright.

"Oh, hi," Becky said cheerfully. "You remember my dad?"

"Of course," Felicity said, smiling.

Taggart, remembering what Becky wanted him to do with this very same Ms. Albright, muttered hello and felt himself blush to the roots of his hair.

"She really is nice," Becky had said on their way out. "Don't you think so, Daddy?"

"Um," Taggart said. He didn't want to think about Felicity Albright. It wasn't good for his hormonal health.

But on the following Saturday morning, they'd had to go into town to buy a gallon of milk and damned if they hadn't run into her again. Taggart didn't understand how they could have run out of it since he'd just bought a gallon two days before.

"Did you finish all the milk?" he'd asked Becky, scowling.

"Me an' Susannah an' Tuck," she'd said. "Isn't that all right?"

What was he supposed to do, ration the kid's calcium intake? They drove to town to the grocery store. Felicity Albright was there buying apples.

"Hi, Ms. Albright!" Becky sang out.

Taggart wished he could sink through the floor.

Felicity smiling at him like that made him want to dig the hole even deeper. And when she said, "My, but Becky has certainly been working hard lately. I can't imagine what must have been the problem earlier," Taggart thought that if he dug clear to China, he still wouldn't be far enough away.

And then there was the Laundromat.

Ordinarily Taggart never set foot inside the Laundromat. He had his folks' old washer and dryer, and they did the job just fine. But Tuesday afternoon when he went to put in a load, the washing machine had gone clunk, clank, sputter.

"What the hell's wrong with you?" he asked it. Not surprisingly, he got no answer, except Becky saying plaintively, "What'm I gonna wear?"

Her clothes—*all of them*—were muddier than he'd ever seen them.

"You said you used to get your clothes muddy when you were a kid," Becky reminded him when she heard his teeth come together with a snap.

"Not all at once," Taggart muttered under his breath. "Come on. I can get the gate welded while we do the laundry."

He supposed he was lucky Felicity wasn't having her gate welded, too. It was bad enough that she was right there, putting her clothes in the dryer, when they walked in the Laundromat door. Taggart stopped and stared.

"Gosh, Dad, look who's here!" Becky said.

Taggart didn't move. Or at least not all of him did. He cleared his throat. "Almost forgot. I gotta see a man about a . . . a cow." He gave Felicity a quick nod, thrust a handful of quarters at Becky and took off for the barber shop hoping to find some male reinforcements.

But Nick the barber only wanted to talk about that goodlooking new schoolteacher. Didn't Taggart think she was somethin'? Taggart's mumbled response caused Nick to lean into him with the clippers. He felt lucky to escape with any hair on his head.

At least when he reappeared in the Laundromat, Felicity was no longer there. He breathed a sigh of relief.

Still, seeing her so many places was eerie. It was uncanny.
It was planned.

A guy only had to look at the sphinxlike smile on his daughter's face every time they'd run into the gorgeous Ms. Albright to know he'd been had.

The last straw came on Sunday morning.

"You want to go to church?" Taggart looked at his daughter, astonished. Becky was no more a fan of long-winded sermons than he was. He figured he and God were on a pretty friendly footing—any guy who faced meeting his Maker as often as a bull rider did, kept his priorities straight—but never once had he gone at the urging of his daughter.

Still, maybe this was part of growing up—taking on a new interest in religion. At least that's what he told himself until he came in from parking the truck to find Becky planted in the pew right behind Felicity Albright!

He stopped right where he was. Then Becky turned around and saw him. She waved enthusiastically. "Dad!" she said in a loud whisper.

He glared. But once she'd got his attention, Becky turned around and sat, head bowed, eyes closed in presumably pious contemplation. Her devoted pose was only ruined by the fact that he could see her biting her lip to keep from grinning.

Taggart wanted to bite her head off. He wanted to take off and never look back. But there were people coming up behind him, waiting for him to move, and so finally he walked down the aisle and slid into the pew next to her. His fists clenched on top of his thighs as he stared straight ahead. He ended up staring directly at the back of Felicity's beautiful blond head.

He could, of course, have closed his eyes. He tried. That was worse.

It gave his imagination full rein. It hauled up every fantasy he'd spent the last couple of weeks trying to keep at bay. It spread all the lovely golden hair out on a pillow—*his* pillow—and encouraged him to run his hands through the curly, silken tresses.

He had told himself he didn't like blondes—not after Julie. But Felicity's hair wasn't the cool silvery platinum that Julie's had been. It was a deeper, warmer, burnished golden color. Julie's hair had always made him want to reach out and stroke its almost shiny smoothness. Felicity's, on the other hand, made him want to tangle his hands in it, to tug its gentle waves, to thread his fingers through it, to explore its softness. He wanted to explore the softness of her—all of her. In his dreams he had.

And in his mind he was going to right now—in the middle of church—unless . . .

He jerked open his eyes and sucked in a desperate breath.

Big mistake. Unless that soft lilac scent was some newfangled incense the minister was using, it was Felicity's scent he was breathing in.

He tried holding his breath. Also unwise. He couldn't hold it for an hour. And when he finally did have to breathe he took such a desperate gulp of air that Becky whispered loudly, "'S matter? You sick?"

Taggart jerked back and shot his daughter a hard glare. She knew damned well what the matter was! And if she didn't understand the specifics at her age, she could guess.

Felicity turned her head. He could see her face in profile now, the soft curve of her cheek, the slight tilt of her nose. If she turned much farther, she'd see him sitting right behind her. He could well imagine the look she'd give him then.

He'd seen it often enough in the past week—that startled, slightly bemused glance, that softly knowing smile. She didn't really know, did she? The very thought made his blood heat.

Did she think he was trying to follow her the same way Becky had been? God help him.

"Let us pray," the minister intoned.

Taggart did. Fervently. But if God heard anything he said about wanting to be cool, calm and disinterested, He certainly didn't give any indication. Maybe God didn't listen to liars, Taggart thought grimly, for as devoutly as he seemed to be asking for deliverance from the temptation of Felicity Albright, so equally determinedly did his eyes seek her out and his mind come up with scenarios better played out anywhere other than in church.

He squirmed, wondering if there was any way to get out of here without Felicity Albright seeing him. There wasn't.

Worse, at that very moment, the Reverend Mr. Wilson decided that loving one's neighbors began with getting to know them.

"Look around you! Greet your Sunday morning neighbors," he exhorted them, waving his arm to encompass them all.

And the next thing Taggart knew he was staring into Felicity Albright's startled eyes. Would she look at him like that gazing up from a pillow?

Oh, jeez. He grabbed her outstretched hand and shook it.

It was even softer than he remembered. Or maybe he was simply more aware of the callused roughness of his. Jerking his hand back, he stuffed it into the pocket of his jeans.

"Morning," he muttered.

Felicity smiled. "Good morning, Mr. Jones. Taggart," she corrected herself. Hearing his name on her lips sent a shiver down his spine. God, it was worse than being fifteen again. What had Becky done to him?

"Lovely day, isn't it?" Felicity went on.

"Lovely," he managed, strangled. He didn't usually have trouble talking to women. Usually he could charm the socks right off them—and other things, too, if he so desired. And there he was again, with his thoughts winging off in a definitely nonspiritual direction.

Felicity held out a hand to Becky. "And good morning to you, Miss Jones," she said with a smile. "Have you had a good weekend?"

Becky nodded eagerly. "We got a new bull! Sunfish! He's really mean. Fer-ocious! You wanta come see him?"

Felicity blinked. "Well, thank you. I—"

Taggart considered stuffing a hymnal in his daughter's mouth and was grateful that, before Felicity could answer, Reverend Wilson had moved on to the sermon.

Becky tugged on his hand. "Sit down, Daddy! Everybody else is sittin' down."

So they were. Mortified, Taggart sat.

Reverend Wilson embarked on a rambling discourse about loving your enemies and being kind to the people who tried to do you ill. "It isn't easy," he told them. "Not easy at all."

Taggart figured that it was a damn sight easier than loving your daughter when she was trying to manage your love life. He glowered. Becky sat in pious justification, ignoring him.

The minute the service was over, he didn't give her a chance to renew her invitation. He grabbed her hand and bolted for the door—only to be trapped by Reverend Wilson, who wanted to inquire about his parents.

"Haven't seen you in a while, Taggart," he said easily, grabbing Taggart by the hand and shaking it heartily. "We've missed you. Missed your parents, too. How are Will and Gaye?"

"They're fine." Taggart tried to free his hand. The Reverend hung on.

"Good, good. How do they like it down in Bozeman?"

"A lot," Taggart assured him, trying still to ease out of the minister's surprisingly strong grip. "They'll be back for a visit one of these weekends. I'm sure they'll come by to see you."

"I'll look forward to it. You tell them we miss them," Reverend Wilson commanded him. "We don't get such a lot of new people moving in that we can spare them. Except of course, Fred's lovely niece—" He reached around Taggart to snag someone else's hand and draw her over. "Have you met our new parishioner, Miss Albright?"

Only thirty or forty thousand times, Taggart thought desperately. In person and in his dreams. His gaze met Felicity's, and he saw that she was laughing.

"I teach his daughter," she explained to the minister, still smiling. "And we've run into each other quite often in town, haven't we, Mr. Jones." Her eyes sparkled with amusement, inviting him to share the humor.

But Taggart was beyond thinking anything was funny. Between her reality and his fantasies he had reached the end of his rope.

"I don't know what you think, but I wasn't following you," he said abruptly. "In fact, I don't want anything to do with you!"

And leaving an openmouthed minister and an astonished Felicity Albright staring after him, he grabbed Becky's hand and took off for the truck.

* * *

"You were rude," Becky said.

Taggart didn't reply. He turned onto the gravel road that led to the ranch house, his knuckles white on the steering wheel. The truck kicked up gravel as he drove.

"I bet you hurt her feelings," Becky persisted.

Taggart stomped on the accelerator. The truck hit a pothole, bouncing him so high he smacked his head. He cursed under his breath and saw Becky grip the edge of the seat in silent desperation. Sighing, he slowed down.

"You could say you're sorry."

"So could you," he bit out. Who had goaded him into it, after all?

His daughter chewed her lower lip. "I only wanted to go to church."

"You only wanted to throw me at Ms. Albright!"

"I wasn't sure she was gonna be there."

"Just like you weren't sure she was going to be at the Laundromat or the grocery store or the library."

"I wasn't," she said stubbornly.

"A trial lawyer might get you off on a technicality like that. Your father isn't buying."

Becky scrunched lower in her seat and gave him a put-upon look which he met with a hard glare. She sighed and looked out the window. The truck bumped along the road. Neither of them spoke again until he pulled up in front of the house and shut off the engine. The utter stillness between them seemed to magnify the mere sound of their breathing.

Finally Becky slanted a quick glance his way. "Sorry." Then she unhooked her seat belt, opened the door of the truck, slid down to the ground and started toward the house. Her small shoulders were hunched, as if she were carrying the world—or her father—on her back.

Taggart sat staring after her until she reached the house. Only then did he get out. He didn't head for the house, but for the stock pens and the "fer-ocious" Sunfish he'd bought the day before.

Pitting his desperation against a ton of bovine irritability seemed a good idea right about now.

* * *

"He said what?" Susannah was clearly horrified when Becky called her on the phone and reported what had happened at church.

Becky repeated it word for word. She tried to tell herself it wasn't as rude as it had sounded, but even she knew better than that. But he was right, it wasn't only his fault. She had pushed him too far.

"Maybe if I hadn't put the wrench in the washing machine and got my stuff all muddy," she murmured.

"Too late. Besides, it might be the best thing that ever happened." Susannah was ever the optimist.

"I don't see how," Becky said.

"Easy," Susannah said cheerfully. "Now he'll have to apologize to her."

Every Sunday night after supper since Felicity had arrived in Elmer, two retired schoolteachers, Cloris Stedman and Alice Benn, had spirited her off to the Busy Bee for pie and coffee.

"Think of it as 'girls' night out,'" Cloris told her cheerfully. "Besides, what else do you have to do?"

Other than grade papers, miss Dirk and, for the past two weeks, daydream about Taggart Jones, nothing at all. So every Sunday night, Felicity had gone.

Until tonight.

Tonight when Cloris and Alice appeared on her doorstep promptly at seven-fifteen, she declined.

"Hot date?" Alice asked, bobbing her spectacles up and down on her nose and looking about expectantly.

"No date," Felicity assured her.

"No man." Alice made a tsking sound. "You need a man in your life, my dear." Both she and Cloris were widows, too, but they'd had long and apparently happy marriages. They thought Felicity should start looking around again.

Maybe Felicity would have—if Taggart Jones hadn't said what he'd said this morning in church. She knew she was foolish to have spent the day dwelling on it. But she couldn't believe how much those few harsh words had hurt.

Used to feeling virtually no interest around any man who wasn't Dirk, she had spent the past two weeks speculating about her hormones' revival where Taggart was concerned. When she'd happened to see him all over town, it had somehow seemed to confirm the rightness of those feelings, as well as being uncanny, but really sort of funny—like their own private joke.

Obviously it wasn't funny to Taggart Jones. *I wasn't following you. I don't want anything to do with you!*

His words had echoed in her head all afternoon. At the time, they'd made her feel like crawling under a rock. Fortunately, she didn't think anyone else had heard except Reverend Wilson and, of course, Becky. She'd managed to laugh it off with Reverend Wilson after Taggart had stormed off, dragging Becky behind him.

It wasn't so easy to laugh when she was alone.

I don't want anything to do with you!

Well, fine. She wasn't exactly keen on having anything to do with him, either—not now.

In fact, she wasn't going to the Busy Bee tonight because, wholly irrationally, she was afraid she might run into him if she did. And if he was there, what would he say this time? She didn't want to know. "It's just that I have lots and lots of papers to do," she said vaguely.

Cloris and Alice muttered a little, but then took themselves off. Felicity watched them until they reached the end of the walk. Their heads were together, discussing her, no doubt. Too bad. She needed a little time alone tonight—a chance to lick her wounds.

She went back and sat down at the kitchen table to face a stack of papers. What she'd told them about having papers to grade had been nothing but the truth. She sat down and forced herself to get on with them, but her mind kept wandering, kept remembering, kept hearing Taggart's hurtful words. She was almost relieved to hear a knock on the door an hour later.

Cloris and Alice must be back, bringing her a piece of pie, unwilling to let her miss the fattening part of the evening, even if she declined to accompany them.

"You didn't have to—" she began as she opened the door.

It wasn't Cloris. Or Alice.

It was—heaven help her—Taggart Jones.

Four

And he looked, for all the world, like he'd just come from a bar fight.

"What on earth happened to your face?"

He actually looked startled at her question. He lifted a hand and touched his raw cheek and partially closed right eye almost absently. "This? Nothin'. Just a little run-in with a bull."

"A bull?"

A tide of color crept above the collar of his blue chambray shirt. His mouth twisted wryly. "That mean ol' one Becky told you about, remember? He did what you should've done to me."

"What's that?"

"Kicked me in the ass. Knocked me on my head. I was rude to you this morning. I've come to say I'm sorry."

Felicity stared at him, astonished. If seeing Taggart on her doorstep was unexpected, his apology was even more so. She became aware of her heart hammering just a bit too quickly and deliberately sucked in a slow, careful breath. All she could think was that a woman could get lost in the green depths of Taggart

Jones's one good eye. He was looking at her steadily, waiting for a response, she guessed.

She felt a little giddy. "Thank you. I . . . appreciate that."

They stared at each other. He swallowed. So did she. His swollen eye blinked shut.

"Are you sure you're okay?"

"Fine. It's an occupational hazard. Don't worry about it."

But Felicity couldn't help but worry. She wasn't used to occupational hazards like his. Sitting on tacks and finding the odd frog in one's desk drawer didn't compare. "You ought to put ice on it. Come in here and I'll give you some." She opened the door wider, and, after a bare second's hesitation, he came in.

"Sit down." She didn't stop to think that the room seemed suddenly smaller, closer, warmer. She nodded toward the chairs at the table. He dragged out a chair and sat. She went to the refrigerator and took out a tray of ice cubes, thumping it on the counter to crack them into smaller pieces. Then she put the cracked ice in a plastic bag, wrapped it in a thin dish towel, and handed it to him.

He took off his hat and she noted his recent haircut. It made him look younger, more vulnerable. Or maybe that was the black eye and scraped face.

"You seem to have a little experience with this sort of thing." He set his hat on the table and pressed the makeshift ice bag against his eye.

Felicity wiped her palms on her jeans. "I had brothers. And once my husband broke his foot—"

"Husband?" Taggart's gaze jerked up. He looked around as if he expected to see Dirk in the doorway.

"He died two years ago," Felicity said quietly.

"Oh." Taggart let out a slow breath. "I'm sorry. I didn't know."

"I don't advertise it. It's just . . . there. Like you . . . and your . . . wife." The shuttered look that came over Taggart's face the instant she said the words made her regret them.

"Ex-wife," he corrected.

"Ex-wife," Felicity repeated. "Sorry."

"Not as sorry as I am." He said the words so softly she barely heard them. He didn't look at her, but kept his head down, the ice pack pressed to his eye.

He must have loved her a lot, Felicity decided, and thought for the first time that there might be a harder way to lose a spouse than to a sudden, unexpected death. Wouldn't it be worse to feel rejected? Unloved?

She wanted to go to him, to put a hand on his shoulder, to touch his hair, his cheek. To offer comfort. She wrapped her arms tightly across her breasts, squelching the notion.

"It was . . . kind of you to come and apologize. You didn't really need to. I don't blame you for being a little . . . testy. It must have been a shock to see me right in front of you in church after seeing me all those other times." She gave an awkward little laugh.

Taggart raised his one good eye and met hers. "A bigger shock than it ought to have been."

"What do you mean?"

"I mean I should've realized about all that following Becky and Susannah were doing."

"What about it?" Felicity looked at him, confused.

"We were being set up."

"Set up?"

"By a pair of scheming girls." Taggart dragged the ice bag down his face, then looked at her over the top of it and said flatly, "Becky reckons you'd make a fine mother for her—and a wife for me."

Felicity was grateful she was clutching the back of one of the chairs. Otherwise, she might have sat right down on the floor. She stared at him, astonished.

"A wife! *That's* what they were doing?" She felt her cheeks warm. His face was red, too, and not just from the ice. Felicity thought about all the times in the past two weeks when Becky had turned up in those very same places with her father in tow. She thought how odd it was, what a small town they lived in. She hadn't connected it, but Taggart had known! No wonder he'd dragged Becky off after church today. No wonder he'd said what he had!

"Oh, my," she said now.

Taggart lifted his head. "Oh, my, indeed."

Flustered, she sat down, then bounced up again, feeling somehow that she was contributing to an excess of familiarity by simply seating herself in her own kitchen. She did a lap around the tiny room, picked up the dish cloth, put it down again. "Oh, my."

"Don't worry. I set them straight. At least I thought I had." He shrugged. "Judging from church this morning, I didn't do a very good job."

"Whatever would make them think that we..." Now her cheeks were burning!

"Susannah, I'd bet," Taggart said grimly. "She got her folks together a couple of years back."

"They were separated?"

Taggart shook his head. "They weren't married. Noah didn't even know Susannah existed."

Felicity goggled. "Didn't know?"

"Not till we got in an accident two Christmases ago comin' back from the National Finals. We got smacked by a semi on the Interstate near Laramie in a snowstorm."

Felicity shuddered. "Were you badly hurt?"

"Concussion. Broke my leg. Once I came around and they got things sorted out, I got to come home pretty quick. But Noah punctured a lung and hurt his knee and wrist and shoulder. So he ended up in Laramie doing physical therapy over Christmas. He knew Tess—she's a nurse—'cause he'd recuperated there once before. He reckoned maybe she'd take him in again, so he showed up on her doorstep—" he paused "—and met Susannah."

"Tess hadn't ever told him?"

"She didn't figure he'd want to know." Taggart gave an awkward shrug. "They hadn't parted on the best of terms. There isn't much future if one of you is goin' down the road all the time." His mouth twisted wryly. "Guess I should've figured that out for myself. Anyhow, Susannah talked her mother into letting Noah stay. Just for Christmas, you understand. But, well... Noah wasn't about to let her go again, and eventually they got together, happy as pigs in—" He flushed and broke off. "So, I figure it went to her head and now she and Becky are convinced they can do equally well for me. And you."

"Not your... ex-wife?" She was careful to get it right this time.

"No, thank God." His tone was fervent. Maybe he didn't love her anymore. Maybe he was getting over it. Like she was getting over losing Dirk.

Was she getting over losing Dirk?

Certainly Felicity had never felt as intensely aware of any man since Dirk's death as she did of Taggart Jones. But *marry* him? That was a little drastic.

"Have they done this before?" she asked cautiously.

"Never. And they won't do it again, I promise you."

She smiled. "I'm sure they were only...trying to help. They're young. They'll realize before long that you want to pick your own wife."

"I'm not in the market for a wife." His tone was flat and hard, brooking no argument.

"Oh." Felicity felt oddly deflated. "I see."

Something in her tone must have made him take notice. "Not that you wouldn't be a great candidate if I were," he said quickly.

She gave him a faint smile. "Thank you. I think."

"Hey." His own smile was rueful. "Can't seem to stop sticking my foot in my mouth, can I?"

"Don't worry. I won't be coming after you with a wedding ring. Actually," she admitted, "I came up here to get away from matchmaking friends in L.A."

"All the way to Elmer? Wasn't that a little drastic?"

"Well, I didn't see myself staying in Los Angeles, and I didn't want to go back to Des Moines—that's where I grew up. So when Uncle Fred died and left me the house, well, it seemed like fate, I guess." Her cheeks warmed slightly as she thought he might consider her foolish, but a glance told her that he was simply listening, not judging at all.

Encouraged, she went on. "I remembered how much I loved it here. I spent a summer here with my mom when I was ten— helping Uncle Fred put out his paper, going hiking in the mountains, riding horseback, picking berries—they're all part of my fondest memories. And so—" she shrugged "—I came."

"And?"

"I love it."

"Love it?"

"I do." And as she said the words, she knew firmly and fully that they were true. She'd been living in what had amounted to a holding pattern all the while she'd stayed in Los Angeles after Dirk had died. Perhaps at the time she'd needed to.

But she needed to no longer; in fact, she needed to be somewhere else, to *grow* somewhere else. Elmer.

"Good for you," Taggart said after a moment. His voice was a little gruff, and he looked at her only for a moment, then stared away into space.

"Can I get you a cup of coffee or something?" Felicity asked. She felt hesitant, not wanting to break the tentative rapport that seemed to be developing.

Taggart's eyes focused on her once more. He blinked as if he was suddenly aware of the intimacy of their surroundings and of the possibility that his daughter might be already busy picking out Felicity's engagement ring. He set down the ice pack and stood abruptly. "Nope. Thanks, but I've gotta get going."

"I won't try to marry you tonight," Felicity said lightly, forcing a smile. "If that's what you're worried about."

Taggart flushed. "Sorry. I just . . . don't want you to get the wrong idea . . . thinking I'm trying to . . . you know." He shrugged awkwardly.

"I know," Felicity said gently.

"I really do have work to get done."

"Teaching bull riding?"

"Not tonight. Paperwork. An ad to put together. Some correspondence."

"For your bull-riding school?"

"Yep."

"What's it like, teaching bull riding? I can't imagine."

"Fun. Challenging. I've got some two-day schools. Some three. Some five."

"And what do you teach? How, I mean?"

"We go over fundamentals—the way the bull moves, the way the rider is supposed to move. How to get your head screwed on straight. Bull riding is a mind game as much as a strength game. You're never really stronger than the bull, so you have to succeed some other way. You have to understand that and go with him."

Felicity was fascinated. "How did you get started?"

"It was just something I did. I won a ribbon ridin' a sheep when I was five. Mutton bustin' they call it. Then I started on steers, and when I was in high school, broncs and bulls. Kids hereabouts do that. It's not all that rare. I was good at it. I liked the bulls the most. I was never much for sittin' still."

No, she could see that. She could see it in his daughter, come to that. "But teaching?"

"I like that better than riding most of the time." A smile turned up the corners of his mouth. "I like figuring things out. Helping guys make the best of themselves. They won't all go on and be world champs. In fact, damn few of 'em will even go pro. But what they learn, they can use in whatever they do."

"What do you mean?"

"Confidence. The ability to focus. The determination to do something hard and follow through."

"Yes, I see." At least she was beginning to. "And there really are enough hopeful bull riders around for you to do that full-time?" She flushed at her nosiness. "I'm sorry. That's none of my business."

But Taggart didn't seem to mind. "I teach maybe fifteen schools at home a year. I do about the same number on the road. Noah does the same with bronc riding. It works out."

"I'm impressed."

He shifted from one foot to the other, looking embarrassed. He tugged on his hat. "You oughta come out sometime."

"Maybe I will." She smiled at him.

He swallowed quickly and took a step backward, then gave a quick, jerky nod. "Well, good. Now, I really gotta get goin'." He started for the door.

Felicity rose and followed him. "It was...kind of you to come."

"Had to, after what I said this morning. I was an ass."

"You were embarrassed."

He grimaced. "Ain't that the truth?" Then he grinned and shook his head. "Reckon I'll have to keep a firm hand on that girl."

Their gazes met, clung, electricity arcing once more. Felicity nodded. "Reckon you will."

* * *

"Didja see her?" Becky asked. They were in the truck driving home from Susannah's, where Taggart had dropped her while he'd gone to apologize—not that he'd told her so. "Have to see a man about a bull" was all he'd said.

"See who?" he asked his daughter now.

"You know who." Becky looked up at him unflinchingly, waiting for a reply.

"I saw her," Taggart admitted, his tone gruff.

Becky got a small smile on her face. Then she gave a little bounce. "I like her. Lots."

Trouble was, so did he.

Her daydreaming about Taggart Jones should have abated. Realistically, she told herself, there was no point. The man had out and out said he didn't want another wife. But then, she wasn't really in the market for a husband, was she?

Of course not. And besides, these were just dreams. They didn't require confirmation in reality. They were, by their very nature, fantasies—unrelated to real life.

Whatever they were, Felicity had a ton of them. Every sleeping moment. Almost every waking one.

It was because she'd been emotionally dead for so long, she reassured herself. It was healthy. Promising. It meant she was waking up to live again, thinking about the future, about moving on.

Mostly, though, she was thinking about Taggart Jones.

Perversely, she no longer saw him everywhere she looked. In fact, he might as well have dropped off the face of the earth.

She should have taken it for the message it undoubtedly was: that he wasn't interested in her. He was annoyed and embarrassed by his daughter's actions. He'd been embarrassed and ashamed of his own, and he'd done what needed to be done to put things right. End of story.

Still, Felicity looked for him. And when she didn't see him, she asked about him.

"Taggart Jones?" Cloris said.

"Oh, my, yes. Of course we know Taggart." Alice's face was wreathed with a smile, and she gave a little giggle. "Isn't he just the sweetest boy? Always was."

Cloris sniffed. "Bit of a devil, if you ask me."

Alice made a tsking sound. "You're just saying that because of the cow pie, and you know it."

"Cow pie?" Felicity was agog.

Cloris pressed disapproving lips into a thin line. "Don't ask," she said, folding her hands in her lap and giving Alice a quelling look.

But very little, Felicity had begun to realize, quelled Alice Benn. She just giggled and said, "Well, it was rather funny."

"You," Cloris pointed out, "didn't sit in it."

"Oh, dear." Felicity stifled her own giggles as she imagined the very proper Cloris as an unsuspecting victim of a well-placed cow pie.

Cloris gave them both a steely glare, but even as she did so, Felicity detected a glimmer of amusement in the older woman's eyes.

"As I recall," Cloris said tartly, "his daddy made it a little difficult for him to sit down a day or two after. I suppose he didn't turn out too badly," she allowed after a moment. "He seems to have done rather well with that little girl. She's in your class, you say?"

"Yes." Felicity told them about Becky coming to school in spurs.

Alice laughed heartily. Even Cloris cracked a smile.

"Chip off the old block, isn't she?" Alice said. "Why ever did she wear them, do you suppose?"

"She's her father's daughter," Cloris said dryly. "What other reason does she need?"

Which was a fortunate comment because it saved Felicity from having to give the real explanation. She had no intention of telling them it was a matchmaking ploy. Even though neither of them had commented today on her need for a man in her life, last Thursday evening, when she'd had dinner with Alice at her house, the entire conversation had focused on the vital statistics of both of Alice's unmarried grandsons.

"You could do worse, dear," Alice had told her.

"I'm not really interested," she'd said, so she certainly didn't want them getting ideas about her and Taggart now!

She wondered if his eye was still black and swollen, if his cheek was still raw. She remembered the briefest touch of his callused fingers on hers when he'd taken the ice pack. In her fantasies his touch lingered.

". . . distracted this evening, dear," Alice said.

Jolted, Felicity tried to follow the conversation. Both older women looked at her indulgently. She flushed. "I'm just about to start a new project with the children," she lied. "And I've been thinking about that."

"*More* projects?" Cloris's brows arched. She wasn't quite sure about this "project" nonsense. A little old-fashioned reading, writing and arithmetic never hurt anyone, she told Felicity. Felicity had assured her the children got that within the projects, but she could tell Cloris wasn't convinced.

"This one's about families," she said. "Occupations. I want the children to begin thinking about the way their parents earn a living—what skills it takes, how they began to learn those skills as children, how they might already be learning skills themselves."

Not bad since she was making it up as she went along. A curriculum committee with its nose in every teacher's classroom would have a fit about her improvisation. But the more she thought about it, the better it sounded. She'd often told Lori that her California students had no idea what their parents did all day while they were at school. And they lived, in many cases, so far away from the places their parents worked, that they had no sense of how their parents contributed to the life of the community. It would be easier to make the connection in Elmer. It would be good for the students—and good for the parents.

And, incidentally, it would allow Felicity to watch Taggart Jones teach his students how to ride a bull.

"You don't mind, do you?" Becky asked. She had on her innocent waif look, the one he knew was designed to make him give in. She stood looking up at him while he flipped pancakes for their breakfast.

He sighed. "No, I don't mind."

He did. But how could he possibly tell her that Ms. Albright wasn't welcome to observe a session of bull-riding school tomorrow afternoon? Especially when he'd all but invited her himself.

"It's for school," Becky informed him. When he raised his eyebrows in doubt, she added, "We're doin' occupations. 'What keeps our valley alive,' Ms. Albright calls it. We're makin' a documentary."

Taggart's brows lifted even higher. He didn't even know Becky knew the word *documentary*, much less what it meant.

"We're writing the script, and she's doin' the videotaping. Showing what our parents do. Then we're gonna do voice-overs, an' when we get done, we'll have a real movie."

It didn't sound like school the way he remembered it. He was reluctantly impressed. But he still wasn't sure he wanted Felicity Albright hanging around his bull-riding school. He'd had a hard enough time putting her out of his mind this past week. Now that he could imagine her in her house, at a table, leaning her cheek against her palm as she listened to him, smiled at him, it was all that much easier to imagine her other places—like in his bed. He'd made sure he didn't run into her again. But even the "out of sight" business wasn't as successful as he'd hoped.

He slid the turner under the pancakes on the griddle and scooped them onto Becky's plate. "Eat," he told her. "I'll run you up to the bus. We're late."

They wouldn't have been if he hadn't burned the first two batches. It was because she'd kept prattling at him, telling him all about what Ms. Albright had done this week—the stories she'd told them about growing up in Iowa, about living in Southern California, about traveling around Europe with her husband. Her husband, according to Becky, had been a concert cellist.

"That's a very accomplished musician," Becky informed him.

He sure as hell didn't think it was a calf roper.

When he dropped Becky off at the bus stop, he didn't go right home. He stopped the truck on a rise overlooking the pasture. He sat there, letting the engine idle as he stared at the bulls. His pride and joy, bread and butter.

He tried seeing them through the eyes of a woman who'd been married to a cellist, a woman who'd traveled around Europe on her holidays, a woman with golden wavy hair and a smile that made the ice around his heart begin to melt. He tried to imagine what she'd think of a man who rode them for a living—who even went so far as to teach others to ride them.

He didn't have that good an imagination. Until he remembered how Julie had come to see him.

Then he gunned the engine and headed home.

Even though she had a rough idea of what Taggart must do, Felicity didn't quite know what to expect the morning she showed up for bull-riding school. Surely they didn't sit in rows and listen to lectures and raise their hands to ask questions, did they?

What she saw when she opened the door to the "classroom," which was a steel-sided building beside the barn, was a sea of cowboy hats. Black and white and ivory, wool felt and straw, they topped the heads of more cowboys than Felicity had ever seen in one place in her life. Where, she wondered, had they all come from? There must have been twenty at least.

"Twenty-three," Taggart told her later.

But right then she couldn't see him behind the hats. She could hear his voice, though, easy and confident over the sounds of boots on wooden flooring and the clink and rattle of the rowels of twenty-odd pairs of spurs. It was a sound Felicity recognized all too well.

She'd have looked around for Becky, but she knew where the little girl was—right beside her. She had been since Felicity had arrived ten minutes before.

"What are they doing?" she asked as she watched them show Taggart their spurs.

"He's seeing if they're too sharp," Becky said. "You don't want to hurt the bull. You just want 'em to grip with. And he's gotta make sure they got the right kind of spurs, too."

"Right kind?" A spur wasn't simply a spur?

"They got big dull rowels on 'em, see?" Becky pointed to a pair that one young cowboy had in his hand. "Not little ones like bareback riders use. Bronc riders use little ones, too. An' the rowels spin free on theirs, too, 'cause they gotta mark their horses out."

There was obviously a whole specialized vocabulary here that Felicity didn't have a clue about.

"I see," she said, and was determined she was going to before the day was out.

She shouldn't really be spending a whole day on one parent. She'd spent an hour with Lonnie Gilliam's dad in the hardware store. She'd spent another with Sylvie Sorensen's mom, who cut hair. She'd spent at most four hours with Damon Kerrigan's parents, who were wilderness outfitters, watching them prepare for a week-long expedition, taping them packing gear, buying food, going over safety regulations, tying flies and discussing topographical maps.

Surely she'd get enough of Taggart Jones on tape in an hour or two to satisfy the needs of the classroom documentary. Of course she would. But she wouldn't satisfy herself.

Besides, it was Saturday. Her day off. She could do what she liked—even if it happened to be watching one of her student's fathers teach cowboys how to ride a bull.

There were plenty of chairs, but no desks in the classroom. There was also a large-screen television and a barrel sort of contraption braced by two long poles and upholstered with foam padding and a carpet remnant. The poles rested on the ends of a pair of tables. Felicity looked at it warily. It was clearly a nonmechanical surrogate bull.

This was how he taught bull riding? She took a seat at the back of the room and waited until the cowboys had finished milling, the spurs had all been checked, and things were starting to settle down. When the men sat down, she glimpsed Taggart in the corner of the room.

He was examining a braided rope one of the cowboys had handed him. He said something, and in reply the man lifted his left hand. Taggart shook his head. The cowboy grimaced, then shrugged.

"What's the matter?" Felicity asked Becky, needing an interpreter already.

"He musta had a right-handed bull rope," Becky said matter-of-factly. "An' he rides left-handed."

Felicity stared at her, nonplussed. She'd heard of cowboys telling tall tales. But, "a right-handed bull rope"?

She heard a laugh behind her and turned to see Noah. "When you grip the rope, you want the braid working away from the way your hand will turn so it will flex, but not give, see?" He borrowed a rope from one of the cowboys standing nearby and demonstrated. "It's easier not to get hung up, and it gives you better traction and grip."

Felicity looked skeptical, but she took the rope when he handed it to her, then let him wrap it around her fingers the way she would hold it if she were on the back of a bull.

"Turn your hand," Noah said. She did. It slipped. "Now the other." He wrapped it the same way. "Turn," he commanded. She did, and saw at once what he meant. She looked at him with wide eyes.

"Lots of guys ride a bull for the first time at one of the schools. They learn, just like you have, from the ground up."

Felicity figured that most of them would be learning from the bull down before long. She knew she would be! It would have been a treat to simply sit back and watch, but she knew she had to justify her presence, so she got out her video camera.

"Are you teaching today, too?" she asked Noah. He dropped into the chair beside her and stretched his long legs out, crossing his boots at the ankles.

"No. We alternate weeks usually. I shoot the video for Taggart while he works with his guys, and he shoots for me while I work with the bronc riders. When we give schools on the road, though, we usually try to go together at least some of the time. Although lately, with Tess being so far along, Taggart's been going alone and so have I. That way one of us is always home."

"You're good friends." That was abundantly clear.

Noah nodded. "We went down the road together for a lot of years. You know whether you can depend on a guy when you spend that much time with him. Taggart's as good as they come."

There was a quiet certainty in his tone that told Felicity as much as his words about his opinion of the man who was now moving to the front of the room. She picked up the video camera, and, as he began to talk, she began to shoot.

More went into riding a bull than Felicity had ever thought. Taggart didn't simply talk about the care of the equipment— glove, rope, resin, bell, spurs, boots—he showed by his very meticulous preparation that this was serious business. Twenty-three hats nodded at every point he made, everything he said.

Felicity listened intently, which she was sure he was aware of, though he gave no sign. Everyone was aware of her. Taggart had even fielded a few teasing remarks about her presence.

"Gonna get the pretty lady on one of them critters, Taggart?" one brash young cowboy asked.

"Ain't one of those bulls gonna buck her off," laughed another, even more brash.

Taggart's gaze leveled on him with the precision of a battery of guns taking aim. The cowboy flushed and looked quickly away. "Sorry, ma'am," he said to Felicity. "No disrespect intended."

Felicity, who had heard plenty of far more disrespectful things on California beaches, gave him a small nod.

Taggart, point made, nodded, too, then turned his attention to the videos. "Watch these guys. These are guys who do things the way they ought to be done."

Then, with each ride, he stopped the tape and pointed out the correct position. "See here how he's movin' up and forward when the bull does? See the way he's bent into the thrust? And now—" he moved the video forward a few frames "—look at the way he's movin' back to meet the kick."

The hats nodded.

"The mechanics are the same for everybody," he went on. "That's the physics of riding. Gravity and balance and the weight of the body in motion. But style, well, that's different. That depends on each guy personally, his build, height, flexibility, aggressiveness." He grinned. "That's what makes me, me. It's what makes Tuff, Tuff—and Ty, Ty. But the mechanics don't change—and that's what we're gonna be working on here."

He got on the makeshift bull and showed them each move in slow motion. "Build muscle memory," he told them. "Practice. Over and over. Break it down into single tiny movements and work on each one."

Felicity watched, entranced, as he showed them how. She understood exactly what he was telling them about muscle memory. It was what Dirk had trained his fingers to do. He'd played passages over and over, broken pieces down into manageable bits and committed them to the memory of his fingers—exactly the same way Taggart did with bull riding.

"Right, then. Ready to get on and put some of this theory to work?" Taggart asked them at last.

There was a general eager murmur of assent, a scraping and shoving back of chairs, and a jostling toward the door as the hats stampeded toward the bucking chutes. Felicity stood up, too.

Taggart crossed the room and came toward her. "Seen enough?"

She smiled. "Not nearly. I'm fascinated."

He rolled his eyes. But he didn't object when Felicity followed him and Noah and Becky out to the arena. The cowboys had gathered by the chutes. Felicity hadn't taken the time to go up close when she arrived. Now, for the first time, she came within arm's length of a snorting, glaring bull.

It didn't matter that he was on the other side of a metal fence gate. It didn't matter that he was in the chute and she wasn't. She could sense his power, his irritation, his desire to make roadkill out of the cowboy who would settle onto his back.

She stopped where she was.

Noah laughed. "Want to ride?"

"Not on your life." She looked doubtfully at the young men who were clustered around the chutes, wondering at their sanity.

"He's a nice one," Becky told her.

"Nice?"

"We rank them," Noah explained. "He's an easy ride."

He didn't look easy to Felicity. "If you say so."

Becky hopped up and down. "Are you gonna ride, Daddy?"

Felicity looked at Taggart, horrified. She hadn't even thought of that. Now she remembered his black eye and scraped cheek. He'd broken ribs before, Becky had told her. And dislocated his thumb. And got kicked in the knee. And had a groin pull. Some men had died. She knew that, too. She looked at him.

He was looking at her.

"Ah, go on. Ride," Noah said, grinning. "You know you want to."

Still Taggart hesitated.

"We'll pick up the pieces." Noah winked at Becky and Felicity. "Just kidding."

Becky giggled.

Felicity looked at Taggart, her eyes wide and worried.

Taggart looked back. Something passed between them—something Felicity couldn't quite define. Challenge? Determination? Daring? Pride?

Taggart nodded his head. "All right," he said. "I will."

Five

———

Taggart never rode bulls in his schools.

It distracted his students from what they were there for even though they thought it was cool. It distracted him. He was there to teach them what to do, not show off. He'd already proved what he needed to prove.

Hadn't he?

Apparently—if the gnawing in his gut and the nibbling at the edges of his concentration were anything to go by—he hadn't. Not quite.

Besides, distraction seemed to be the name of the game where Felicity Albright was concerned. Taggart hadn't been single-mindedly focused on the job at hand since he'd known she was coming to watch.

He'd be moving bulls or putting together his videos or going over his notes, and the next thing he knew he'd be thinking about Felicity's gentle smile or the way she ran her fingers through her hair. His fingers itched to do it, too.

Don't think about it, he told himself. *Don't think about her.*

It shouldn't have been hard. He was a whiz at mind control, at focus, at seeing only what needed to be seen and doing exactly what he needed to do. If he'd controlled his attention two years ago in Vegas the way he was controlling it around Felicity Albright, he'd have been a cow pie on the Thomas and Mack Arena floor instead of the world champion bull rider of the year.

He had focus, all right. And right now, every bit of it was on her! He'd been aware of her every movement since she opened the door to the classroom that morning. He'd done his damnedest to ignore her, barely letting his gaze light on her when she came in with Becky on her heels like a faithful herd dog.

She didn't matter to him, he assured himself; she didn't have spurs for him to check or a bull rope to look over. She wasn't the issue he needed to concentrate on. Still, he was aware of her; it felt almost as if the very air pressure in the room had altered the moment she'd come in.

He was a professional, for heaven's sake. He was being paid good money to teach twenty-three guys everything he could about bull riding in two short days. If he spent twelve or thirteen hours with them each day he would barely scratch the surface even if he—and they—focused every minute.

Why the hell had he said he'd ride a bull?

Because he was thinking not with his head, but with that gender-specific equipment tucked away in his Wranglers. Damn it.

"C'mon," he said, raising his voice now. "Let's get moving!"

He got a cup of coffee from the urn on the small card table outside the arena. Then, cup in hand, he climbed over the fence and headed toward the chutes where Mace Nichols and Jed McCall, Tuck's uncle, were running in the bulls.

Out of the corner of his eye he could see Felicity sitting at the top of the small set of bleachers he and Noah had built last summer. Becky sat with her. Noah, who was supposed to be on the platform next to the bleachers manning the video camera, was in fact sitting on Felicity's other side, chatting. Taggart watched as she leaned toward Noah and nodded at some comment he made. He said something else and they both laughed, then looked in his direction. Irritated, Taggart jerked his gaze away.

He climbed up on the chute gate and began talking to his students. Most had ridden bulls before; some were just there for a refresher course—a "tune-up," Noah called it. But there were three complete rookies, guys who hadn't so much as touched a bull.

"Gotta start somewhere," Taggart said, giving them a grin of encouragement. They all looked white-faced with apprehension.

He went over the fundamentals slowly and carefully. How to resin the rope and glove, how to put the rope on the bull, how to hook it under, then pull it up tight, how to make the wrap tight and secure around your hand. He fitted them with protective vests, which wouldn't save them from all injuries—in bull riding, he reminded them, it wasn't a matter of *if* you get hurt, it was *when*—but they could save a life. He knew cases where they had, and other sadder cases where they could have, if only the cowboy had been wearing one.

While he talked, the bulls clanked against the metal railings, kicking and blowing. One of the new guys muttered under his breath. Taggart stopped to sip his coffee. A bull reared up, hooking his horns at a cowboy on the top rail. He scrambled out of the way.

"Some of 'em come right straight up," Taggart cautioned. "Don't be gettin' in there till you're ready to ride."

"Yes, sir." This particular cowboy looked as if he was ready to hit the trail.

Taggart smiled at him. "You ready?"

It was one of the novices. He shook his head.

"These bulls are a little too snuffy for a first-timer, anyway." Taggart ranked them according to how tough they were to ride. Mace and Jed had filled the chutes with number-two bulls, animals to challenge the better riders. "How 'bout another volunteer. Jason?"

A lean, tough kid from a ranch near Dillon, Jason Dix had been to one of his schools last year. He'd also competed in the Montana State High School Finals Rodeo in both bronc and bull-riding last summer. Jason scrambled over the railing to put his rope on the first bull. One of the other experienced cowboys dropped down into the arena to fish it out and pass it up to him. The new guys got out of the way.

One by one, they rode. Jason and three or four others lasted more than a few seconds. Some barely got out of the chute. Taggart cheered all of them on, regardless, watching intently, never once letting his gaze drift over to where Felicity sat.

"That it?" Mace asked when the last of the new guys had been dumped in the dust.

Taggart hesitated. "Run in Sunfish."

Mace raised his eyebrows. "Who's that good?"

"Me."

Felicity had watched all the other cowboys ride with a combination of nervousness and exhilaration. She felt no exhilaration now—only terror. She knew, of course, that Taggart Jones rode bulls. She knew he'd been champion of the world. He was, without question, a man who would be good at what he did.

But even though he was wearing a vest, even though he knew the risks he was taking, she still didn't want to look. He could get killed.

Of course, she didn't say that. Who would she say it to? Becky? His daughter sat next to her, bouncing up and down with excitement.

"He never rides bulls in his schools," she'd informed Felicity only moments before. "He must be doin' it for you!"

He didn't have to do it for her, Felicity wanted to tell him. Please God, that was the last thing she wanted him to do! She should have left. She had enough tape of Taggart Jones to more than suffice for the part he would have in the class's video. She could leave now.

If she could make her feet work. If her legs would hold her. They felt like jelly. Felicity stayed where she was. She tried to look away, but a heretofore untapped morbid fascination gripped her as Taggart braced himself above the bull's back, his booted feet on the rails on either side of the chute, and prepared to lower himself down.

Felicity swallowed, her mouth as parched as Death Valley. Her fingers clutched the video camera in a death grip.

"Aren'tcha gonna tape him?" Becky asked. "You oughta tape him."

Felicity's hands shook. She'd taped other cowboys—most of whom had barely got out of the chute, one or two who'd made it through a kick and a thrust and spin. "I've got quite a lot on tape," she told Becky.

"Not like my dad."

No, not Taggart. Felicity sucked in a breath. Maybe Becky was right. It might help. Maybe if she watched him through the viewfinder it would seem like nothing more frightening than a car chase on television. She picked up the camera and pressed her eye against the viewfinder. Her finger found the zoom, and she closed in on him. She saw him, feet still braced, pull up on the rope once, test it, then haul it tighter yet. Then he pulled his glove out of his belt and tugged it on. Then he rubbed his gloved hand up and down the rope before beginning to wrap his hand.

The rails were in the way, so Felicity couldn't see his hands. She didn't care. She watched his face, the tight look of concentration that came over him as he settled down and shoved himself forward into his hand, the flat press of his lips and the bunch of his jaw. The mike picked up the mutters of half a dozen chattering cowboys. Taggart didn't make a sound. He shifted, centered, stilled, then nodded his head.

The gate swung open and the bull exploded into the arena.

Felicity jerked the camera aside, unable to zoom back fast enough to catch more than the whirl of color and movement that was Taggart and the bull. She clutched it against her breasts, forgotten. Her heart pounded as she watched the intricate dance of man and animal—the arch and thrust, the kick and leap of the bull, complemented by the movements of the man who sat on his back.

Having just seen twenty-three young men flung around like sacks of potatoes, then stomped and kicked in the dirt, Felicity had asked herself why anyone would do such a thing.

She got a glimpse of the answer now. It wasn't a simple answer, either; she saw that, too. Riding a bull the way Taggart was riding this one was both a test of courage and a celebration of life. It was a walk on the edge of disaster—a balancing act of beauty and terror, of power and grace. Well done, it was a compliment to both the man and the animal. It showcased the animal's force, his cunning, his strength, his determination.

And it pitted them against a far weaker, but equally graceful, wily and determined human being. It was a ballet of stimulus and response, a waltz of twist and spin.

It lasted an eternity. It lasted eight seconds. Maybe ten. There was no whistle, no buzzer. Only at last, a ducking movement on the part of the bull, a hard backward thrust of his hind feet, a jerk of his head, a sideways twist, and Taggart's compensating moves weren't quick enough or far enough. He slipped, his free hand dipped. He tilted, loosed his hand, and as the bull bunched and thrust forward again, Taggart leapt away.

He landed flat on his back in the dust. As the clownishly dressed bull fighter distracted the animal, Taggart scrambled to his feet and sprinted for the fence, hauling himself up and over. Then, without so much as a pause, he took his cup of coffee back from the cowboy who'd been holding it, took a long swig and, finally, glanced over at her.

Felicity was conscious suddenly of clutching the camera so tightly against her that it was making grooves in her arms and pressing her breasts flat. She eased her grip, opened her mouth and sucked in a deep draught of dusty, bovine-scented air.

"Good goin', Daddy!" Becky yelled. She looked up at Felicity, a grin on her face. "Didja see him? Didja see that? Wasn't he great?"

"Great," Felicity echoed hollowly. She felt the strength beginning to return to her legs. "I—think I ought to go."

"Go?" Becky's face fell. "You can't! You gotta watch the rest of it. You don't really wanta go, do you?" She looked beseechingly at Felicity.

No, Felicity thought, *she didn't.* "All right," she said. "I suppose I can stay awhile longer."

Becky beamed. "C'mon." She bounded down off the bleachers, leaving Felicity to stumble after her. Felicity's knees wobbled as she climbed down, just as if she were the one who'd spent all that adrenaline, not Taggart.

"What next?" she asked Becky.

"Critiques."

Critiques, Felicity found, meant that the entire brigade trooped back to the classroom, where Noah handed the camera over to Taggart and flashed Felicity a grin before he disappeared.

"Gotta go check on my missus," he said as he headed for the door. "You wanta come and play with Susannah, Beck?"

Becky edged closer to Felicity. "No. I wanta watch."

Noah's eyes met Felicity's over Becky's head. He grinned and gave her a wink. "I'll be back."

Felicity sat in the back of the classroom with Becky at her side and listened to Taggart painstakingly critique each bull ride, playing the video in slow motion, freeze framing it to point out the good moves, then to point out where things began to go wrong.

"You don't hurt yourself with one big mistake usually," he told them. "It's a buildup of little ones. They're cumulative. A little slip here where you don't quite get set right—" he pointed at the frozen cowboy on the television screen "—and that throws you off for the next jump. Next thing you know you're flat on your butt in the dust."

The hats nodded. Taggart moved on.

"Here now," he said to one cowboy. "You got good form here when you come out of the chute, but watch—" the video moved forward a couple of seconds "—now you're sittin' back on your pockets. You're givin' him all the advantage 'cause you're off-balance and you can't grip him with your calves. This isn't bronc ridin', Danny. You don't have to mark 'im out."

There was a general chuckle at Taggart's reference to the bronc and bareback riders being required to have their spurs high on the horse's neck when they came out of the chute. The cowboy called Danny grinned, then nodded. "I'll get 'im next time."

Felicity watched Danny's ride end with him being flung hard against the arena fence. She winced at the sound of the clang and rattle when he hit. And he was going to do it again?

Apparently they all were.

Felicity was sure they'd take a break, instead they headed back to the arena for another ride. Only after they'd all taken another turn did Taggart call a break. Tess Tanner and Jenny Nichols had set up a table under the trees and were cooking hot dogs and ladling up bowls of chili. She was so hungry the enticing smells rendered her weak in the knees.

That was what did it, she assured herself, not a lean and still slightly dusty Taggart Jones, climbing over the fence, coffee cup in hand, to smile crookedly and say, "How about some lunch?"

After a quick meal, during which half a dozen guys came up to ask him specific questions, Taggart herded them back to the classroom and went over each cowboy's ride with the same thoroughness that he'd used on the first ones. Becky lost interest and went out to follow Jed and Mace around.

Felicity stayed in the classroom, watching the videos. She began to understand what Taggart was talking about when he pointed out somebody being too far back or being told he looked like he was waving to the crowd. She saw the little mistakes that led to bigger ones. She saw how the mechanics that Taggart was talking about came into play time after time after time.

It was past five when he finished the critiques and said, "Not bad. You're gettin' the hang of it." He gave them a thumbs up, and Felicity, glancing at the clock, started to pack up her things.

"Okay—" Taggart clapped his hands together "—back to the chutes. Get on, get set, get out. We got plenty more stuff to cover 'fore we go home tonight."

Felicity stared, dumbfounded. But the cowboys, some of them stiff, a few of them bloody, all of them far dirtier and dustier than they had been in the morning, hauled themselves to their feet and headed out the door.

Taggart followed. "You don't have to stay," he said to her.

"You're going to go through another entire round?"

"Yep. I'd rather do this in three days. But we've only got two, so we're makin' the most of it. Shut off the light when you leave."

Felicity got to her feet. "I'm not leaving."

They didn't finish until almost ten—after another full round of rides and critiques. Then Taggart showed a video of little kids riding sheep. The oldest couldn't have been more than five or six. One of them, the last one, was barely three or four.

"See that?" he said as the little girl clung and rode...and rode, then waved her hands in triumph when she landed on her bottom and bounced up again. "That's my daughter."

There was a giggle from the doorway. Felicity and those cowboys who still had enough cooperative muscles to turn around looked back to see Becky grinning.

"What's the word?" Taggart asked her.

Becky grinned even more broadly. "If I can do it, you can do it," she told the assembled cowboys. "See you tomorrow."

He wouldn't see Felicity tomorrow. She wouldn't be there. He was surprised she'd stayed so long today.

Taggart felt uncomfortably flattered. Julie's attention span where his bull riding was concerned was barely longer than the eight seconds it took for a qualified ride. He didn't try to kid himself that she would have been happier if he'd stayed home and taught bull riding instead of going down the road.

Marrying him had been a whim. Most girls felt the same way about even dating him. He didn't inspire commitment. Most women weren't as crazy as Julie, though, so they never even pretended otherwise. And frankly, he'd never cared. Which was why Felicity Albright made him uncomfortable.

She made him want to care.

He wished she'd left. He'd thought maybe seeing him ride the bull would send her on her way. Some women got passionate about men who did stupid, dangerous things for a living. He seriously doubted that Felicity was one of them.

But she hadn't left. In fact, her mind didn't even seem to be wandering. She didn't paint her nails or read a magazine the way Julie had. She taped him talking in the classroom, making him feel awkward and like he ought to be dropping pearls of wisdom instead of just talking about where to put your free hand so you had the best balance and why you shouldn't try to second-guess bulls. That was bad enough. But at other times, she'd simply sat watching him. And that was worse. He felt like he ought to wipe his face or check to see if his fly was open.

He'd tried not to look at her. She wasn't important.

Yeah, sure.

He knew that for the lie it was Sunday morning in the middle of reviewing mechanics and talking about role models, when the door opened and Felicity slipped in.

She gave him a quick, almost guilty, smile and slid into a seat at the back of the room. He kept right on talking, but his voice felt suddenly stronger, as if his earlier words had been mere rehearsal, as if it was Felicity he'd been waiting for.

Get your head on straight, he commanded himself. *Focus, damn it.*

He tried. "Take your time," he told his students. "Practice. Every day. Every movement. Even if it takes you ten minutes to get something right once, get it right. Give your muscles something to remember. I can teach you the movements. But I can't teach you try. That you get on your own, from inside. You put the two together and you'll be just fine." He looked at them steadily. "Now, let's go ride some bulls."

They were out the door almost before he finished speaking. Felicity, however, moved more leisurely, as if she was waiting for him, and he fell into step beside her, trying to mask the eagerness he felt.

"You're back?" He made it a question.

She favored him with a smile. "I couldn't stay away."

He tripped over his boot. "What?" He shot her a quick sideways look.

Her smile widened. "I love watching you teach. You're so good at it. You inspire them. You make them understand. They're getting kicked and stomped and run over in the dust and they love every minute of it."

He laughed. "Yeah, well, nobody said bull riders were real bright."

"Some of them are very bright, and all of these guys are very dedicated. The dedication they're showing is something that will carry over no matter what they go on to do."

He nodded. "That's the point, really. If they learn how to apply themselves to bull riding, there's no reason they can't do it wherever they want."

"Dirk used to say the same thing to his students," she said softly. "My husband," she added, when Taggart's head jerked around.

"I remember." The comparison surprised him. He didn't think he could possibly have anything in common with her cello-playing husband.

"He loved teaching, too. He was good at it, just like you are. He reached different people, but he taught them the same basics. You're really very much alike."

They'd reached the arena by that time and she left him to climb up and perch at the top where she'd sat yesterday. He started to climb the fence. His foot slipped and he whacked his chin on the top rail.

"Been walkin' long?" Noah grinned from his spot on the platform.

Taggart swallowed blood from biting his tongue. He tugged his hat down and tried the fence again. "Come on," he shouted to the first cowboys in the chutes. "Let's go."

There were four steps up to the entrance to the classroom. By six o'clock Sunday evening very few cowboys were taking them two at a time. Two or three even had to use the handrail to pull themselves up. The grimaces Felicity saw on their faces betrayed feelings their words would belie—if anyone asked how they were, which no one did.

They were fine. They were cowboys.

Would that Dirk had seen the same dedication from his cellists, Felicity thought. One or two had actually shown a similar determination, but she doubted if even they would have turned as a group to shush the EMT talking loudly while he sewed up one guy's leg in the back of the classroom after the final bull ride Sunday night, just so they could hear what Taggart was saying.

Felicity knew she had never seen that kind of dedication among any of her students! She'd never, ever, heard one of them say, "Be quiet so I can hear Ms. Albright explain how to divide whole numbers." Not once had any of them said, "Shut up! I want to hear Ms. Albright tell us the difference between proper and common nouns."

Ah, well . . . maybe if she taught them how to ride bulls.

And they had hushed and paid attention when she got them interested in studying the history of the valley they lived in, when she told stories of the Indians who'd hunted there and the white settlers who had come to ranch and to farm. That meant something—just like Taggart's instructions meant something to these guys—and when she was lucky, she got in the division and the nouns through the history they read and the stories she told.

He ended with a pep talk that she taped so she could listen to it over and over. "Dedication is what it's all about," he told them. "You got to want it. If you want it, you can make it happen. And that's what you have to think about—making it happen, believing it can happen." His gaze moved slowly from one cowboy to another, connecting with each and every one of them. Then he nodded slowly. "Believe in yourself. If you don't, you not only won't finish, you won't even start."

Felicity sat in the back and watched the cowboys straighten up slowly. They were aching, all of them. Sore muscles, scrapes, abrasions abounded. They'd ridden five or six bulls in the past thirty-six hours. Every fiber of their bodies hurt. But they straightened anyway, they sucked in their breath, nodded their heads.

Taggart watched them; his eyes traveled over them once more and a slow smile spread across his face. "You all got what it takes," he told them. "Good luck."

She stayed till the bitter end. The last cowboy had climbed into his truck and rumbled down the road, and Felicity was still sitting in the classroom watching the video he'd left running. Taggart stood in the doorway, watching her, just enjoying the view. She was writing something in a notebook, her head bent, her wavy golden hair obscuring his view of her profile, but he didn't need to see it to know exactly what she looked like.

Suddenly she seemed to realize he was there because she turned guiltily, then jumped to her feet.

"I was just . . . digesting."

"Enough to give you indigestion, was it?"

She smiled, shaking her head. "No. It was wonderful. You were wonderful."

He dipped his head. "Thanks, but I don't do it alone. Noah, Mace, Jed, Jenny, Tess. There's a whole lot of people involved. I'm only as good as my cast and crew."

"And bulls."

He grinned. "Them, too."

He waited while she packed up her camera and put away her notebook, then started to slip on her jacket. Automatically he reached around to help her. Easing it up her shoulders, he touched her hair. It was as soft as he'd imagined it. He let it curl through his fingers, rubbed his thumb against a strand. Then, reluctantly, he stepped away and followed her out into the cold October night.

A canopy of stars and a sliver of moonlight showed in the ink black sky overhead. It was the sky he saw every night, and yet tonight it felt different, new.

Felicity's shoes made a scrunching sound on the gravel as they walked down the path toward her car, and Taggart was suddenly aware that they were alone. Becky had long since gone in to bed, and Noah had just left for home. In fact Taggart could see his taillights disappearing over the rise right then.

It was just him ... and Felicity Albright.

A shiver slid up his spine that had nothing to do with the cold. All sorts of ideas began swirling in his head—ideas as inappropriate as they were unlikely. It was Becky's fault, he told himself. If she hadn't said ...

But it wouldn't have mattered what Becky had said. He was perfectly capable of appreciating a beautiful woman without the help of his daughter. The question was, What was he supposed to do about it?

The answers that occurred to him made his tongue stick to the roof of his mouth. He couldn't seem to say a word.

They stopped beside her car.

She turned to him, so close he could smell the soft flowery scent of her shampoo. He sucked in his breath. She smiled up at him. "Thank you for letting me come."

He swallowed, shifted from one booted foot to the other. "My pleasure. I hope Becky didn't do too much arm-twisting."

"Becky had nothing to do with it."

"What did?" The question was out of his mouth before he had a chance to stop himself. *Your job is to react, not to think,* he told his bull riders. Yeah, sure, he thought desperately now. And look where that gets you.

"Because I wanted to come," Felicity said quietly. "I was enthralled. I wanted to watch them learn." She hesitated. "And I wanted to watch you."

Before he could think *or* react to that, she went up on her toes just enough to brush a quick kiss across his lips. Then she opened the car door, got in, started the engine and drove away.

Taggart was still standing there five minutes later when her taillights vanished over the rise. His knuckles rubbed against his lips.

For the first time in memory he was scared.

Six

––––––

She should *never* have kissed him.

Heavens above, what *had* she been thinking?

Well, she hadn't. That was precisely the problem. She'd simply reacted—to the man, to the moment. And now she felt like a robber stealing off in the getaway car, half expecting the propriety police to be blaring their sirens and racing down the road after her to haul her in.

She had *kissed* the father of one of her students!

Where were her ethical standards? Where was her professional demeanor? Where were her brains, for goodness' sake? Men were the ones who were supposed to be governed by their hormones, not women.

How sexist is that, Felicity Jane? she asked herself.

Very. And it obviously wasn't true, either. God, what must Taggart be thinking?

She could feel her cheeks burning even now, twenty minutes later. She rolled down the window of the car and let the cold night air nip at them as she drove. But she'd need a blizzard to take the heat out of them after what she'd done.

"A cold shower for you, kiddo," she prescribed as she skidded around the turn that took her off the gravel road and onto the paved county highway.

But even the icy shower she forced herself to endure when she got home didn't totally relieve the burn of awareness or the memory of Taggart's lips against hers. It had been so fleeting she couldn't imagine why she could still feel their touch.

She told herself he wouldn't think anything of it. Taggart Jones had surely been kissed by plenty of women in his life. She doubted there was a man alive who'd been a world champion bull rider and never been kissed. One more wouldn't faze him a bit. He probably wouldn't even remember she'd done it.

And she might have made herself believe it if she hadn't glanced in the rearview mirror—and spied Taggart, standing stock still right where she had left him, staring after her, his fist pressed against his mouth.

"Fool," she called herself. "Idiot."

She went to bed and tossed and turned, hugged her pillow, then thumped it and tried to get comfortable. There was no comfort. She got up again and turned on the light. She would read. Reading would take her mind off things—off Taggart.

She reached for the book she'd left on the bedside table. And saw Dirk.

Of course every night she saw Dirk. She had his picture right where she would see him the last thing before she turned out the light and settled in. It was habit. It was ritual. She smiled at him, told him about her day, touched his smile, said goodnight. Every night.

Except tonight.

Tonight she hadn't even remembered. She'd shut off the light and flung herself onto the bed, her mind whirling so fast she couldn't think, only feel.

"Oh, Dirk." She reached for his picture, then sank down on the bed, holding it, cradling it in her hands, looking down at him. "Dirk, what am I doing?"

He smiled at her the way he always had, supporting, encouraging. Dirk had always been the more even tempered of the two of them. He'd always rolled with the punches far better than she had. He'd been able to look at the bright side when Felicity had only seen the gloom.

She wondered what he'd see if he looked at Taggart Jones.

"I think you'd like him," she told Dirk's portrait. She ran her thumb lovingly over the glass that protected his smile. "I do."

But she shouldn't have kissed him.

She lay back on her bed and drew her pillow tight against her breasts. "Should I apologize to you?" she asked. It wasn't Dirk she was talking to.

She didn't have a chance.

"He's out of town," Becky told her when he didn't come to the screening of the tape about the parents' occupations. The students had all made invitations and taken them home. Most of the parents came. Only Sam Bacon's and Teresa Faraday's weren't there. And Becky Jones's father.

"He's got a school in Oklahoma this weekend. He left last night," Becky told her glumly.

Felicity had chosen a Friday to show the tape. Now she wished she'd picked a Monday or a Tuesday. Any day when Taggart would have been able to come. Two weeks had passed since her foolish kiss—long enough for her to be convinced that he'd forgotten—even if she couldn't possibly. She remembered it—*him*—more intensely than she wanted to. It was an odd feeling. Unrequited. Not at all the way she'd felt about Dirk. Except the interest. The interest was definitely there.

"He can stop by and see it after school someday," she told Becky. "You tell him."

But when Becky came back to school on Monday, she said, "He wants to know if you'll send it home with me so he can run it in our camcorder." She didn't look particularly happy about the request. Felicity wasn't, either, but she could think of no reason to refuse.

She hoped he might bring it back himself. He didn't. She thought he might ring her up and say he'd enjoyed it, that she'd done a good job with his bull-riding part. She had, damn it.

But another week went by and she never heard a word.

She shouldn't have been surprised. He'd made it quite plain that he didn't want to get involved. Not that she was desperate to get involved, either, she tried to tell herself.

But the more time passed, the more she knew that wasn't entirely true. She had mourned Dirk for two years. Somewhere deep inside, she loved him still; always would. But she was alive, too. She wasn't even thirty years old. She wanted to love again.

And even though she told herself it was pointless, she wanted to love Taggart Jones.

At least she wanted to *try* to love him. Or even get to know him! Was that asking so much?

Apparently Taggart thought so. He clearly had no burning desire to get to know her. Her only consolation was that he would have to show up for the class production about the history of the valley. Wouldn't he? No, he wouldn't. Not if he could manufacture a commitment elsewhere.

Unless she got him to make a commitment to her.

He wasn't cooperating, Becky told Susannah. "Whenever I try to talk about her, he changes the subject. He won't even listen to what I do in school anymore. And he hasn't seen her in weeks! He won't go into town, either."

"Really?" Susannah said, a tiny smile playing at the corners of her mouth. "Good."

"Good?" Becky muttered. "I needed pencils and we could've got 'em at the grocery store, but he says we have to wait till we go to Bozeman. And he's grouchy all the time, too."

"Even better."

"Easy for you to say."

Susannah just laughed. "He wants to see her, but he's afraid to."

"You think so?" Becky said doubtfully.

"Of course." Susannah's tone was airy. "That's the way men are."

"You did *what?*" Taggart, who had been stacking bales of hay when Becky appeared bearing news, turned and glared at his daughter.

She stood her ground. "I told Ms. Albright you'd videotape our local history projects on Wednesday. She asked," Becky added when his glower deepened.

"She just came up to you and said, 'By the way, Becky Jones, I wonder if your dad would mind videotaping for us on Wednesday?'" Taggart wasn't usually sarcastic to his daughter. This time he couldn't help it.

She bobbed her head. "Yes. She did! You don't think I'd tell her you would, do you? Without askin' you?"

"Yes," Taggart replied dryly.

Becky flushed, then gave him a long-suffering look. "Well, I didn't. You're too crabby lately. I'd never do that. You'd yell."

"I would not."

"You just did."

He flushed and rubbed the back of his neck. "I'm just... surprised."

And dismayed. He didn't want to go to Becky's class. He didn't want to see her teacher. He saw Felicity Albright often enough—in his thoughts, in his fantasies, in his dreams. He relived the kiss Felicity had given him so often you'd have thought it was the last one he was ever going to have.

It was sure as hell the last thing he'd ever expected.

He chewed at his lip now, aware that just thinking about it made him remember the feel of Felicity's soft mouth brushing his. It had made his nights long and his body hungry. He'd wanted to see her again—and knew he didn't dare.

He'd stayed on the ranch since, not risking even one trip to town. He'd got Tess to pick up groceries for him or he'd driven down to Bozeman. He'd had Noah take in the horse trailer to get the broken brace welded. He'd only left to drive straight to the airport, and even then he'd been looking over his shoulder.

He knew, of course, that he couldn't avoid her forever. But he figured he'd have his libido under control by the time he had to go to Becky's parent-teacher conferences. He wasn't there yet.

"Why me?" he demanded.

Becky shrugged. "Most parents don't know how."

"Noah does."

"Yeah, but—" Becky scuffed her toe in the dirt, then studied the mark it made.

"But what?"

She slanted him a look. "You want me to hafta tell Susannah you're chicken?"

"*What?*"

"Afraid of Ms. Albright." She spelled it out for him.

Taggart's jaw worked. He scowled at her, furious. "*I'm not afraid of Ms. Albright!*"

"Well, what would you call it?" Becky's stubborn little chin jutted out, dared him to come up with a better description.

He cussed under his breath. He fumed and muttered. He took off his hat, slapped it against his thigh, then jammed it back down on his head. "Oh, hell, all right."

Felicity wanted everything to go perfectly. She wanted the kids to say their pieces with the same enthusiasm she saw every day in the classroom. She wanted the parents to be proud of their accomplishments. She wanted them to think she was doing well by their kids. She wanted Taggart Jones to smile at her.

He was coming; Becky had said he was. She'd tried to search the little girl's expression for some idea of how Taggart felt about being asked—as if she didn't know—but Becky gave nothing away.

Now Felicity wiped her palms on the sides of her navy pleated trousers and tried to get the kids to focus on their math assignment. But most of them were far too keyed up at the notion of the program they were putting on for their parents in half an hour.

Felicity was keyed up, too. Because Taggart was coming.

"I hafta go to the bathroom," Geri Tibbets interrupted for the fourth time that morning.

So do I, Felicity thought, but she could hardly keep running to the lavatory. "Go on," she said.

"Can I get a drink? My mouth is dry," said Randy Decker.

So is mine, Felicity thought, but trips to the drinking fountain were equally unacceptable. She wet her lips with her tongue. She was always slightly nervous before such events because she wanted everyone to do well, and it was, of course, out of her control. But she couldn't ever remember being quite this strung out before.

"He's here," Becky said suddenly in the hush that fell over the classroom, and Felicity looked up to see Taggart in the doorway. It was the first time she'd laid eyes on him since she'd kissed him. If she'd entertained any notion that she might have got over her awareness of him in the ensuing weeks, she was glad she hadn't counted on it. She was as aware as ever. More so. Her eyes went right to his lips. Heat burned her cheeks.

She managed a smile. "Ah, Mr. Jones. I'm so glad you could come and help us out."

"Ms. Albright," he drawled. "I wouldn't have missed it for the world."

Becky and Susannah exchanged significant looks, which caused Felicity's cheeks to heat even more. Her mouth felt like it was filled with cotton. "We appreciate your willingness to help out."

"My pleasure." He didn't look as if he'd been dragged here kicking and screaming. But he didn't look all that happy to see her, either. Probably he hadn't given her a thought. Probably he'd just been busy, not avoiding her.

Oh, Felicity, you ninny, she chastised herself. *You silly dreamer.* Her feet landed back on the ground.

Taggart slipped off his backpack. "Brought my own camera."

"I have one."

"Easier to work with the one I know." He was opening the pack even as he spoke, not really looking at her, just taking out the camera and battery with the same quick competence with which she'd seen him tighten a bull rope or climb a fence with a cup of coffee in his hand.

The children, who had quieted when he came in, began to murmur again when they saw him begin to get the camera ready, as if they suddenly realized why he was there. The nervous chatter rose to a crescendo. Felicity cleared her throat.

"Girls and boys," she said in her best soothing tones. "Having someone come into the classroom is no reason to forget what we're supposed to be doing. We just have a few more minutes to get things in order before our presentation, so let's use them wisely. Moaning doesn't help, Lizbeth, Randy." She singled out the two most vocal grumblers. "I think most of you know Becky's father, but if you don't, this is Mr. Jones. He's going to help us today by making a videotape of our local history presentation."

Talking steadied her, made her focus on the children, on her job—not on Taggart. As she talked, the experienced teacher in her took over.

Taggart settled into the back of the room, fiddled with the equipment, gazed into the viewfinder, followed her with it. That was a little unnerving, but Felicity soldiered on, doing her best to ignore him. But out of the corner of her eye she watched him.

She saw Tuck McCall sidle up to where Taggart was perched on the back counter—still flouting the rules, Felicity thought, smothering a smile.

"Hey, Taggart."

"Hey, Tuck. How's it goin'?"

"Okay." Tuck stood watching while Taggart panned the classroom, catching Felicity looking at them. Quickly she looked away. "Can I come watch your school sometime?"

"Sure. Got one in two weeks. You gonna learn to ride?"

"Naw. I wanta draw them bulls."

Taggart lowered the camera. "Draw 'em?"

Tuck nodded gravely.

Taggart gave Tuck a slow smile. "Well, sure, why not?"

Tuck grinned. "Thanks. Me an' Jed saw a coyote last night. Up near Flathead." He launched into a tale that amazed Felicity. It was the most voluntary conversation she'd heard from Tuck McCall. Having tried to converse with his uncle and guardian Jed McCall about participating in the "parents' occupations" video to no avail—"Can't," Jed had said—she had suspected Tuck's reticence was genetic.

Perhaps she'd been wrong.

She had no more time to consider the notion, though, for more parents were beginning to straggle in.

Most of them she'd met while doing the earlier video. Both Tess and Noah Tanner arrived, Noah carrying a little boy and Tess waddling alongside, so pregnant that Felicity found herself hoping she didn't deliver during the presentation. Randy Decker's mom was there. His father, a truck driver, couldn't make it. Neither, not surprisingly, could Jed McCall. Geri Tibbets had a full complement of parents and grandparents in attendance. Sam Bacon's father didn't come, but his mother was there. That pleased Felicity, because she knew Sam needed all the encouragement he could get. He was clever and quick with his hands, but his strengths didn't lie in the area of traditional learning. She'd heard from his teacher last year how little success Sam had had in school. He'd had quite a lot in the local history project. He'd started it rather apprehensively, but by the time they were finished, he was contributing as much as anyone. She was happy his mother would see how well he'd done.

She smiled in Mrs. Bacon's direction. The woman gave her a tight smile in return. A few more parents came in.

Felicity greeted them all, then quieted the kids, nodded at Taggart to start taping and began to introduce the program. "It's important for our children to know something about the world in which they live. The immediate world," she added. "And that means the valley they're growing up in. They need to see themselves as part of a larger context—a process, if you like, of which they are a small but significant part. It's been going on for a long, long time. Eons," she told them, scanning the crowd of proud and interested faces. "And so we'll begin with the geology of the region. Becky?"

Becky, face flushed, got up and walked over to the map she'd labored over so long. Together she and Sam propped it against the blackboard. Felicity held her breath, but the mountains stayed put, and so did the trees and the tiny ski resort stuck in the Bridgers.

"This is where we live," Becky said in a serious, grown-up tone. And then she began to explain how the valley had come to be. She talked about the formation of the valley, the shift in the earth's plates. On cue, Tuck and Sam got up and showed, with pieces of corrugated cardboard, exactly what had happened, how the earth's crust had slipped and buckled. While Becky talked about the inland sea that had covered much of the earth's surface, Tuck showed drawings he'd made of the plant life that had left fossils in the region. Then, when Becky had covered the geological history of the area, she started pointing out things as they were in the valley and surrounding mountains today.

Felicity glanced back at Taggart. He was watching his daughter through the viewfinder. He was also grinning all over his face.

Felicity sent a prayer of thanksgiving heavenward, then turned her attention back to the class.

After Becky, Susannah gave her report on the people who came to the valley, and Tuck showed drawings he had made to illustrate them. Then Sam showed his display of the replicas of artifacts he'd made: the rifle, the bow and arrows, the powder horn, the buffalo horn spoon. He talked, at first haltingly, and then with more enthusiasm, about what he'd learned.

When he sat down, with obvious relief, he was smiling, too. He looked at his mother and grinned. He got another of the tight smiles she'd given Felicity earlier.

Poor little kid, Felicity thought. But she couldn't spare him much more consideration just then, because Randy and Teresa were getting up to talk.

Each group in turn shared the results of their explorations. One group wore costumes that depicted the clothing of the various people who'd lived in the valley at certain times. They explained why the clothing was appropriate to the lifestyle of the time. Another group talked about the animals and birds of the valley, using photos and a record of bird songs and a deer skin.

At the end, Felicity led them in singing a song they'd made up about the valley and the people and the animals who had lived there. Becky, she noted, sang louder than anyone.

Only when the parents had finished their enthusiastic clapping did Taggart stop taping. But when he put down the camera, he was still grinning. For an instant his eyes met hers.

Felicity felt the combined weight of the entire third and fourth grades of Elmer Elementary School slide from her shoulders. She breathed again.

Afterward, parents and children crowded around, looking at each exhibit more closely, talking among themselves and to her. There was excitement in the air. Enthusiasm. Noah and Tess shook hands with her, telling her how much they liked the program, how much they thought Susannah was learning. So did Geri Tibbets's mother and Lizbeth's and Randy Decker's.

Sam's didn't. She was gone almost as soon as the program ended.

So was Taggart Jones.

Felicity hadn't been in any hurry to get through the throng of parents. She didn't imagine she would need to be. Of course, he'd stopped taping, but that didn't mean he was going to leave immediately, did it?

Apparently it did, for when she looked around after most of the parents had disappeared, Taggart was no longer there. The videotape lay on her desk. She picked it up. It was still warm.

Swallowing the lump of disappointment in her throat, she dredged her peppiest smile up from her toes. "You were wonderful," she told the class. "I couldn't be prouder of you. How about an extralong recess?"

The whoops and hollers were deafening.

"If," she said severely, "you can be quiet until I get you outdoors. There are other classes in the building hard at work, and you can't disturb them." They quieted down, and once they had she led them outside for recess. Jenny Nichols stayed outside to watch them while Felicity went back to the classroom.

She needed a little space, a little time to think. Time to recover. Not from the program. But from seeing Taggart come—and go—without a word to her.

She still held the tape in her hand. The product she had asked for. Not at all what she wanted. She lifted the tape to her cheek and pressed it there.

"Felicity?"

She spun around.

Taggart stood in the doorway.

"I was wondering . . . would you like to go out to dinner?"

Seven

He should be minding his own business! He should be getting into his truck and heading home.

He'd done what he'd come for—to see Becky do her presentation, to make the videotape as Felicity had requested. He didn't have any further reason to stick around.

Except to tell Felicity what he'd heard.

It wasn't his problem. It certainly wasn't his business. He'd told himself that all the way out to his truck. He'd even got in and started the engine.

But then, just as he'd started to leave, he looked over and saw Felicity letting the kids out to play. They'd spilled down the steps, hooting and hollering, and she stood there watching them, smiling at them. She'd looked young and innocent and happy.

Then, as he'd watched, her smile faded. She looked lonely, lost, almost, as she ran a hand through her windswept hair. She turned and said something to Jenny Nichols. Then, hugging her arms across her breasts, Felicity went up the steps and disappeared into the building once more.

And Taggart had gone after her.

Where the invitation to dinner came from, he wasn't sure.

He certainly hadn't had to ask her. He'd wanted to. There was that kiss, after all.

Not that he'd asked her because of the kiss! God, he'd been running from that kiss for weeks. But it wasn't working—the running. He was thinking about her all the time. Maybe it was better to see her—eat with her—get to know her. *Get over feeling the way he felt around her.* Yeah, that must've been why he'd done it. Self-preservation.

"It has nothing to do with—with what Becky wanted," he said to her now, not wanting her to get the wrong idea. "It's not a date."

"Oh." And damned if it didn't look like the light went right out of her eyes. Then Felicity straightened and met his gaze squarely. "Of course not." Her tone was brisk, but he felt as if he'd just kicked a pup.

"I didn't mean . . . I wasn't . . ."

"No, I understand," she said quickly. "You're telling me what the rules are because last time I . . . broke them."

He swallowed. "You mean the . . . kiss?" He damn near strangled on the word. "Don't be silly," he said, lying through his teeth. "It doesn't matter. I don't get kissed and tell, if that's what you're worried about. It didn't mean anything," he added, and dared a direct glance at her for confirmation.

She didn't nod. Hell.

He scuffed his toe on the linoleum floor. "You don't have to come," he said gruffly.

"I want to come." Her soft voice pierced the armor he was trying hard to keep up.

Their gazes collided again. Taggart quickly looked away. "Fine." If it wasn't a date, why the hell did it feel so much like one? "I'll pick you up at six."

She folded her hands on the desk and looked at him. "Thank you for making the tape. I really ought to be taking you to dinner."

"This one's on me."

Outside, children shrieked and yelled. Down the hall he could hear chairs scraping and some teacher droning on. That was what he remembered about school, the droning. He couldn't imagine Felicity droning. And what he could imagine he wasn't supposed to be thinking about at all.

He ran his tongue over his lips. "Right. See you then."

"Where are you going, Daddy?" Becky asked. She was perched on the toilet seat lid, watching him shave. It had become something of a ritual over the years, a time to talk, a time to laugh. Sometimes he put a shaving soap mustache on her face and made her giggle. She had one now and was watching him with bright, eager eyes as she swung her legs back and forth, kicking her boots against the porcelain bowl.

He kept his eyes firmly on his own mirror image as he scraped the razor up his cheek. "Out to dinner."

"Can I come?"

"Tess invited you over."

She sighed. "I always go to Tess's."

"And you're going again tonight."

"Where you going?"

Why, he wondered, did they have to play twenty questions? "Down to Livingston. No big deal."

"To the pizza place?" Becky got that desperate, hungry look on her face.

"Not the pizza place."

"How come?"

"Because I'm not in the mood for pizza."

"Are you in the mood for love?"

Taggart's razor damn near slit his throat. *"What?"*

Becky stifled a giggle, but her expression was guileless. "It's a song Tess sings sometimes."

"Oh." He breathed a little easier. Not much. Tess needed to censor her singing material. He grabbed a tissue and stanched the flow of blood from the cut on his neck.

"Who you going with?"

"A friend."

"A *girl*friend?"

"Just a friend." He'd envisioned having this conversation with her one day. But in his version, *he'd* been the one asking the questions.

"A girlfriend," she translated hopefully. Then, stricken by a sudden thought, she blurted, "Not Kitzy Miller?"

Taggart's eyes met hers in the mirror. "What's wrong with Kitzy Miller?"

"Her hair is stiff and her eyelids are purple."

Taggart smothered a grin and lied, "I never noticed."

Becky rolled her eyes. Then she gave a little hop and her eyes grew wide. "Is it Ms. Albright?"

Taggart cut himself again. "Damn!"

Becky, beaming, handed him another tissue. "I'm glad," she said and gave a deep sigh of contentment.

"I didn't say I was going with Ms. Albright!"

Apparently he didn't have to. Everything he did must be transparent to the eight-year-old female mind. He felt hopelessly outclassed and outmaneuvered.

"You're not to make anything out of this," he told her sternly. "I just need to talk to her about a few things—related to school."

"Sure." She looked at him owlishly. "Wait till I tell Susannah!"

Taggart nailed her with his fierce father expression. "If you say one word to Susannah about this, I'll ground you till you're married."

Becky just giggled. Then she threw her arms around his waist and hugged him hard. "Don't worry, Daddy. I won't tell."

Felicity heard his truck come up the street a few moments past six. Running the brush through her hair one last time and praying for the good sense not to do anything rash—like kiss him again—she drew a deep breath and went to the door. She wasn't prepared to have him practically bolt inside the moment she opened it.

"What's wrong?" A wind had come up this afternoon, blowing down from the Bridgers, but Taggart didn't look like the wind had blown him in. He was glancing over his shoulder like he had a posse after him. He jerked off his hat and ran a hand through his hair, then leaned his back against the door. "You didn't happen to mention that you were going out to dinner tonight, did you?"

"Just to Maudie Gilliam."

"And with who?"

"She asked," Felicity said, feeling just a bit defensive.

Taggart groaned.

"I didn't know it wasn't allowed. She brought me some left-over meat loaf when I got home from school. She was going to stay and eat with me, but I said I was going out."

"Figures. And now the whole damn town has ideas." He looked hunted.

"Ideas?"

"About us. You and me."

"I told her it wasn't a date. Well, that's what you said," she reminded him when he groaned again.

"Great. You didn't think that was maybe protesting a bit too much. Jeez. Those old biddies will put Becky to shame."

Felicity sniffed. "Don't be ridiculous. They aren't interested in what I do."

"You see Maudie out there weeding just now? There hasn't been a weed in her yard since World War II. And Mrs. Benn was sitting on her porch with old Horrible Cloribel starin' at me when I drove up the street. Even Sam Eberhardt was giving me the eye. And when have you ever known Sam to rake leaves?"

"Well, I haven't. But I haven't been here long. Who's Mrs. Benn? Oh, you mean Alice. And horrible Cloribel?" Felicity's brow creased. "Not *Cloris Stedman?*"

"It's what we called her in school." Taggart strode over to the sink and pulled back the curtain to peer out the window. It took only a quick look apparently. He let the curtain fall. "I had both of 'em. Cloribel for two years."

"Did you flunk?"

He grimaced. "No thanks to her. She taught fourth *and* fifth grade. I reckoned she didn't think it was enough to make my life miserable for one year."

Felicity grinned. "From what I heard, you made her life pretty miserable, too."

Taggart almost smiled. "She told you about the cow pie?"

"Mentioned it."

"Served her right." He tugged his hat down on his head as if to emphasize his words.

"Alice is very fond of you."

Taggart grunted. "She had a sense of humor. Ol' Cloribel didn't."

"You might be surprised," Felicity said dryly. She lifted the curtain. A convention of neighbors had gathered in the middle of the block, talking among themselves and looking at her house and Taggart's truck. Alice was beaming.

"I'm sorry...about telling Maudie, I mean. I didn't realize they'd all be outside watching. Are you sure it isn't just coincidence?"

Taggart gave her a dark look. "What do you think?"

Felicity thought he was probably right. "We don't have to go."

"We're going. Are you ready?" He looked her over briefly, and a hint of color rose in his cheeks as he took in her eager face. "I guess you are. Come on. Let's go."

The sharp wind had brought cooler weather, so Felicity grabbed her jacket along with her purse, then followed him down the steps and across the yard. She thought he'd head for the Busy Bee, but he headed for his truck.

"We're going to Livingston."

"Oh." Felicity supposed if they went to the Busy Bee, all the neighbors would come, too. It might be good for the local economy, but it wouldn't do much for Taggart's peace of mind. Or for her own. She nodded and got in.

Taggart got in, too, flicked on the ignition and backed around. Then he shot down the street, spraying gravel everywhere.

"Taggart!"

He grinned unrepentantly. "They want to stand in the street, they gotta take what they get."

But he slowed down before he got to where they stood. Still, he stared straight ahead while Felicity waved at them all as he drove past. By the time they got to the end of the street, she was laughing.

"It's insane," Taggart grumbled. "I'm glad I never courted a local girl. I don't see how Jenny and Mace Nichols survived."

"Jenny grew up here?"

Taggart nodded. "She's the same age as my sister, Erin. Jenny and Mace were high school sweethearts." He made a face that told Felicity he didn't think much of the idea. "Mace was always nuts about her. And she was about him, too."

"They seem very happy."

"Happy? I guess so," he said gruffly. "They been married over ten years. More power to 'em, I say."

Felicity heard the strain in his voice. She glanced over at his hard profile. Was he thinking about his own marriage? She didn't dare ask. Instead, after a moment, she turned and stared out the window, watching as cirrus clouds blew east above the Bridgers. The peaks were already capped with snow left earlier in the week.

"Winter's coming," she said softly.

At her words, Taggart seemed to breathe again, and she realized that since he'd made his comment about Jenny and Mace, he must have been holding his breath. His fingers flexed, then loosened, on the steering wheel. "Let's hope it doesn't come too soon. Those clouds aren't a good sign."

Felicity studied them for a moment. In California, except for occasional torrential rains that the drainage system wasn't equipped to handle, or bouts of drought that brought about water-use strictures, she hadn't had to pay much attention to weather. In Iowa it had been more of an issue, but it seemed slightly more predictable than Montana. The year she and her mother had come to stay with Uncle Fred there had been snow on the Fourth of July. And once Uncle Fred had sent her a picture of a picnic in February.

"I should have had one of the children do a section on weather. I could definitely use some instruction," she said.

"Just ask. We'll bore you for hours. Cloribel was big on weather. Actually," he reflected, resting his arm on the window ledge, "I learned quite a bit from her."

"She'd be pleased to hear it."

"She never will from me."

"You aren't fond of teachers."

He slanted a glance her way. "You're pretty damn good. That program today was impressive. I was surprised how much the kids knew."

Felicity was startled, then inordinately pleased at his praise. "They worked so hard. Every chance they could get. People often say kids aren't motivated, but they are if they're interested."

"They were obviously interested. And wired, too. Becky was practically going nuts last night—worrying about getting everything right."

"I hope she slept. I never thought about that."

Taggart grinned. "After thirty or forty drinks of water and bounces up to make sure she had everything written down, she went out like a light."

"I'd hate to have parents coming after me with shotguns!"

"They wouldn't do that." There was a second's pause. Then, "I hope," he muttered.

"What?"

"Nothing." He cleared his throat and flexed his hands on the steering wheel. "The only other time I remember Becky gettin' like that was before the Christmas program last year," he went on firmly. "And then she was just standing in a row singing. The year she actually had a part—as a snowman—I missed it."

"Because of the accident?"

"You know about that?"

"Becky told me a little. It . . . reminded me of Dirk's. One minute everything was fine, the next the world had changed."

His hand left the steering wheel, stealing over to enfold her fingers in a warm, gentle grip. Felicity felt the comfort offered, the kindred feeling. Neither spoke. Taggart continued to watch the road, and Felicity stared out at the clouds beginning to build over the hills to the west. But all her attention was concentrated on the fingers Taggart held in his hand. It felt so good, so right.

"Tell me about when Becky was little," she said after a moment. "What was she like?"

Taggart started to smile. "A trooper," he said. "Becky's always been a trooper. I took her down the road with me, did you know that?"

"To all the rodeos?" She couldn't hide the surprise in her voice. But she was smiling, too, at the thought of this tough, hard man caring enough about his daughter to want her with him all the time.

"Almost all of 'em. Now and then I'd leave her with my folks, but mostly it was her and me and Noah. We went all over." He grinned. "Even went to Disneyland once. Got some of those ears. Guys were callin' us The Three Mouseketeers."

Felicity laughed and settled back to listen. It was the right question to have asked. Talking about Becky was something Taggart did easily and with enthusiasm. Every little girl should have such a father, Felicity thought. The miles passed all too fast.

The wind was equally strong in Livingston. Not surprising. The town had a reputation for being one of the windiest in the West. Now she shivered and wished she'd brought a warmer jacket. But Taggart found a parking place only a few doors down from the old brick building that housed the restaurant, so it didn't really matter.

The dining room was paneled in dark wood, and overhead fans hung from what Felicity assumed was the original pressed-tin ceiling. A long, ornately carved bar with a brass rail and a beveled mirror sat along one wall. Along the other was a row of booths. In the middle and at the back diners sat at heavy oak tables.

"Right this way," the hostess said, and led them to a discreet corner table. The sort of place one put couples who wanted to be alone together. Felicity sneaked a glance in Taggart's direction. His face was impassive. He held her chair for her, then sat down opposite. Felicity picked up her menu, but over it she watched Taggart. All right, she thought, it isn't a date. But then, what is it?

Taggart waited until they ordered before he told her. "I heard something today I thought you should know." His fingers drummed briefly on the tabletop. Then he dropped his hand into his lap.

"Something you heard?" Felicity wondered what could possibly make him take her clear to Livingston to talk about it. "This afternoon? At the program, you mean?"

He nodded. "A couple of the parents were…complaining."

Her brows knitted. "About the program?"

"About you."

"*Me?*" She stared at him.

He shrugged as if he wished he hadn't brought it up. "They're a couple of whiners. Nothin' makes 'em happy, but—" his mouth twisted "—sometimes they can get out of hand."

Felicity looked at him warily. "What do you mean, out of hand?"

"They get a bee in their bonnet about somethin' they don't like, and they want to get rid of it, you know?"

"Get rid of me, you mean?"

His fingers started drumming again. "Not necessarily. I mean, I don't think they're aimin' to get rid of you, exactly. Not yet, but..." His voice trailed off. It was pretty clear to Felicity that if they weren't there yet, Taggart thought they were soon going to be.

"What did they say?" she demanded. "Exactly."

"Well, I can't say word for word, but—"

"You must have a pretty good idea. You asked me out to dinner on the basis of it."

He shoved back in his chair and raised his hands as if to defend himself. "Hey, I just thought you had a right to know."

"So tell me!"

But he studied the tabletop for a long moment before he finally raised his eyes to meet hers. "They said you were playin' games. They said you weren't doing basics. They said the kids weren't learning the right things."

"Not learning the right things? They're learning history! They're learning to read and write and understand how their world works!"

"But not the way we used to."

Her gaze narrowed on him. "You mean if it's boring, it's better?"

"No! Hell, no. I didn't say that!"

"But that's what you're implying."

"*They're* implying. Not me. I think they're full of you know what." He paused. "But—" He lifted his shoulders in a gesture of helplessness.

"But what?"

"But Orrin Bacon is on the school board and—"

"Sam Bacon's dad? He wasn't even there!"

"Elizabeth was. His wife," Taggart explained. "Orrin's probably on the road. Couldn't make it, but—"

"Then exactly how is he qualified to judge my teaching?"

"I never said he was, just said he's doing it."

Felicity felt her mouth open, then close, then open again. A hundred responses crowded her brain. None of this made any sense! "Are you telling me my job is in jeopardy?" she asked him finally.

The waitress came bringing their steaks. Felicity had lost her appetite. She waited, but Taggart didn't reply until the waitress had left. "I don't know," he said, his gaze level, meeting hers. "Orrin's a pretty tough guy to buck. He's got plenty of opinions and he doesn't hesitate to make them known."

"But Sam's doing well!"

Taggart's mouth twisted. "By your standards, maybe."

"By anyone's standards, I should think. He wasn't doing any better with traditional methods! Damn it." Felicity attacked her steak with the desire to cut Orrin Bacon in two. "I can't believe this!" Felicity pointed her knife at Taggart. "Do you know how hard Sam has had it in school? No, of course you don't. And I shouldn't be telling you." Another breach of professional ethics. She went back to sawing her steak.

"I know," Taggart said quietly. He spread his hands when she looked up at him warily. "How could I not? This is a small town, remember? Everybody knows I took you to dinner. I know Sam has trouble in school."

"Well, then, do you know that I'm finally reaching him?"

He shook his head. "No, I didn't know that."

"Because the darling Bacons aren't talking about it, obviously."

"But if you are, why aren't they pleased?"

"I don't know! Because they're perverse. Because they're stubborn. Because they're determined stick-in-the-muds who only want success if they get it their way!" Felicity brought her silverware down with a clatter.

"Hey," Taggart said gently, "careful with the dishes. And don't kill the messenger."

Felicity sighed. "Sorry." She managed a smile, but it was a pained smile. How could the Bacons be the ones complaining? Of all the parents, they ought to be most pleased. "Does anyone else have problems?"

His gaze flickered away for a moment. "One or two. Nothing much."

"What?" She wanted all the cards on the table now.

He shrugged awkwardly. "A couple said the program was...frivolous."

"Frivolous." She repeated the word with deadly calm.

"The costumes and the...I don't know what you'd call it...multimedia approach, I guess. Hands-on, maybe that's the word. They thought it was...unnecessary. They thought the thing on parents' occupations was, too." He gave her a helpless look. "I don't mean I'm agreeing with 'em. I just thought you ought to know. They don't like frills."

She stared at him, stupefied. *"Frills?"*

"They want their kids memorizing things, doing papers, turning 'em in, getting a grade. Going on to the next subject."

"And it doesn't matter if their kids learn anything?"

"Kids *do* learn that way. I did," he added defensively.

"And loved every minute of it, obviously. I remember all those happy stories you told me...about you and Cloribel the Horrible."

He looked uncomfortable. "I did learn from her. I told you that."

"And you so clearly enjoyed every minute."

"I didn't need to."

"Wouldn't you rather have enjoyed it?"

"Of course, but—"

"Then what's wrong with making what they have to learn anyway interesting and enjoyable? Why make them hate it? I believe in what I'm doing. And I think I've made a difference for the better. For all the kids, Sam included. Especially Sam. What are Bacons going to do?"

"What do you mean, going to do?"

"I mean, you're obviously concerned about this. You braved having dinner with me to tell me." He scowled at her wording, but she didn't care. "So what's going to happen? Is he going to shoot me? Run me out of town?"

"Of course not. He can't do either. But he might have the power to see that your contract isn't renewed."

She wanted to say, "So what?" She couldn't, because there was nothing "so what" about it. She cared—far more than she thought she would—about keeping this job. Elmer, in the few months she'd been here, had come to seem more like a home to her than California ever had. It was the place where she'd discovered how to live again after Dirk's death. And to have it threatened right out of the blue—especially when she knew she was doing a good job! Her stomach knotted. So did her fist around the knife.

Taggart watched her worriedly. "I didn't tell you in order to upset you," he apologized.

"I know. I'm sorry. It's just not fair. I thought people were pleased."

"People ought to be," he said firmly. "I am. Becky's a bright enough kid, and she's done well in school—when she's worked," he added wryly. "But she's never liked it the way she has this year. And it's not just because . . . because she thinks you'd be . . . uh, because you'd be . . ." He stumbled, then stopped. "Aw, hell."

"Because I'd be mother material?"

He shot her a glance from beneath lowered brows. "She knows better now. I straightened her out," he said firmly.

"I gathered you had."

She tried to look upbeat, but she must not have done a very good job, because Taggart said, "It isn't that I don't . . . like you. I just don't want to get married."

"You don't have to explain," she said, feeling her cheeks warm.

"Yes, I do. I don't want you to think I'm . . . findin' fault. Like the Bacons, you know?" He looked at her earnestly.

Felicity smiled faintly. "So I won't feel like I'm a complete all-around failure, you mean?"

"Cripes, no, I never meant *that*."

He was flustered now, she could tell, and she knew she had to take pity on him.

"I understand, Taggart. I was teasing."

"Oh," he mumbled. "Yeah." He bent his head over his dinner, sawing doggedly at his steak.

Felicity cut hers, too, and took another bite, but all the while she chewed, she couldn't take her eyes off Taggart Jones.

She knew it was a lost cause. She'd finally awakened to the possibility of having a new man in her life, and the new man she had awakened to had apparently vowed to become Rip Van Winkle where women were concerned.

Still, she watched him. She couldn't seem to get enough of watching him. She'd played her video of bull-riding school over and over again, watching not just the bull rider, Taggart Jones, who was impressive, but the teacher, Taggart Jones, who impressed her even more.

"*You* teach the way I do," she said suddenly.

His head jerked up. "What? What are you talking about?"

"You don't teach your students out of books. You show them things—videos, even—and then you put them on the bulls."

"Because I'm teaching bull riding," he said patiently.

"But it has to do with life. You said so. And I'm teaching my students what they need to know in life, too. I'm teaching them subjects—like reading and history and arithmetic. But more important, I'm teaching them *how* to learn, *how* to find out things later on when they're out of school. They won't bother if they think it's all drudgery. But if I show them that there are alternative ways to learn things—" she was poking her knife at him again, she realized. Deliberately she set it down. But then she looked back up, fire in her eyes. "If I show them ways to learn that they can understand, they'll use those ways in the future. They'll have the tools they need to learn whatever they need to!"

She looked at him, impatient, waiting for a response. He wasn't agreeing enthusiastically, that was for sure.

But finally he nodded his head. "Yeah. You're right."

That was all he said. He wasn't fired up the way she was, but there was a quiet certainty to his tone that was just as good. Better, perhaps, because she suspected she could count on it. Felicity smiled at him, justified.

Slowly, almost reluctantly, Taggart returned her smile.

Eight

———

There. He'd done it. He'd taken her to dinner. He'd told her about the grumblings of Sam Bacon's mother, he'd hinted at the furor he knew damn well Orrin Bacon could stir up. He'd done his duty. He'd even managed a bit of small talk on the side.

After they'd disposed of the Bacons, he'd asked her about her time in California. And then, later, about Europe. "If you don't mind talking about it," he'd said hastily, realizing she might not want to relive memories of trips with her husband with him.

But she didn't seem to mind. In fact, she talked about him quite willingly and at length. Dirk Albright sounded like a damned paragon. But Taggart couldn't dislike a guy who'd built a car out of spare parts as a teenager, who'd spent an entire summer canoeing in northern Canada with his brother, who'd swept Felicity off her feet in junior high by writing her messages in Morse code.

"Love letters," Felicity had giggled.

For a cellist, he actually sounded almost like a regular guy.

Maybe even a fun one. Taggart sort of wished he could have met him. Sort of.

It was obvious how much Felicity had loved her husband. It showed in her face, in her eyes, in her smile, even the wistful one. Part of him wished he'd never brought Europe up—or Dirk. Another part told him it was salutary that he had.

He knew Felicity had had a wonderful marriage, just like he knew he'd had a lousy one. They had nothing in common, see?

He saw. It didn't help.

Because he also saw a woman he wanted. When she told him about traveling to Europe—to Paris and Vienna and Salzburg the summer after she and Dirk had graduated from college, camping and staying in hostels—she made it seem not very different from the way he'd lived, going down the road from town to town. Only a little more exotic. He thought he'd like to see some of those places some day. He said so.

"You'd love it," she told him eagerly, eyes sparkling. They'd finished their dinner and were drinking coffee. It was getting late, and he should be taking her home, but he made no move other than to sit and sip. He even dared look at her now and then for longer than a split second.

"Yeah, I probably would," he said now, reflectively. He wished he could see it all. With her.

But that would never happen, he told himself firmly. Tonight was a one-off. A sort of test. Like riding a bull. He was pitting himself against an unknown force, setting himself up against the temptation of succumbing to Felicity Albright's charms.

He'd needed to. To prove that he could do it—and survive.

And he had. Even though he wanted her more now than he had this afternoon.

Taggart finished his coffee quickly and paid the bill. Then he ushered her ahead of him toward the door and held it open so she could precede him.

Out into the swirling snow.

Snow?

Small sharp flakes stung his eyes as the wind whipped them in his face. An icy north wind bit into him. Oh, yes, snow. Unseasonable, unpredictable, entirely possible Montana snow.

Felicity shivered and turned to him, incredulous. "I don't believe this."

"I do," Taggart said darkly, cursing his lack of forethought. The National Weather Service hadn't said anything about a coming storm, but he didn't need them to have seen the high, fast-moving cirrus clouds that had come over the mountains from the west earlier in the evening. He didn't need them to tell him about the sharp wind. He'd just been too strung out over Felicity to notice. And now he was going to pay.

"Is it...safe to drive back to Elmer in this?" Felicity asked.

Safer than spending the night in a motel room, Taggart thought. "It'll be fine," he promised. "There's only a couple of inches on the ground so far. We can make it." Taking her arm, he steered her toward the truck. He could touch her through her jacket with immunity, he was certain. Well, maybe not so certain. She was so close she radiated warmth as she stumbled along beside him, her head ducked down.

"It won't be bad, will it? It's only October," she said hopefully.

"The worst storm I ever saw was in October," he replied before he thought.

She winced. "Then you think this is going to be a big one."

"Naw. I doubt it," he said, not wanting to make things worse than they already were. "It'll probably let up soon."

"Says the guy who isn't wearing sandals."

He glanced down. Her bare toes were peeking out at him. "Damn!" He bent, reached around and swung her up into his arms.

"Taggart!"

"You'd rather get your feet frozen? Relax. It's only a few feet."

It really wasn't far distancewise. She wasn't even very heavy. Heck, he slung Becky around all the time—not to mention saddles and hay bales and other ranch gear. The trouble was, Felicity didn't feel like any ranch gear he'd ever lugged. She didn't feel very much like his daughter, either.

He cursed under his breath, all too aware of the firm warmth of her body in his arms. Her mouth was so close that her breath warmed his cheek. He turned his head. Even so, he could smell a flowery scent. Lilacs, he thought.

In the snow? Was he losing his mind? Yep. And his composure.

He almost dumped her next to the truck, then opened the door. She slipped in with a grateful sigh. Taggart caught her feet and brushed the snow off her bare toes. They were cold and trembled at his touch. She gave a tiny giggle that sent a shaft of need zinging through him.

He backed away hastily. "There's a blanket in the back of the cab. Can you reach it?"

She was tucking it around her when he climbed in the other side. "You come prepared." She turned a smile on him. Snowflakes glistened on her lashes and shone in her hair like tiny diamonds. He wanted to touch one.

No, you don't, he told himself firmly, sucking in his breath and flicking the key in the ignition. That way lay disaster. He was almost home free.

But he wasn't home yet.

"Got to be prepared in Montana," he said brusquely. "You never know what to expect."

Something else Julie had hated, he reminded himself. "I don't mind cold weather," she'd said, "but some days it's 50 degrees below zero. The next it's 50 above. It rains one minute, then snows the next. And the wind. God, I hate the wind."

Felicity hugged herself. "This is wonderful."

Taggart's head jerked around. He shot her a wary glance. "What's wonderful?"

She was still smiling. "This weather. It's amazing. I love it."

He gave her a sour look. "And when there's a job opening in the Antarctic, you'll take it?"

Felicity laughed. "No, but I'm serious about this. California—where I lived in California, at least—the weather was always the same. You almost never even noticed it."

"Must have been nice," Taggart said dryly.

"It was boring."

"Well, whatever this is—boring it ain't." He put the truck in gear and eased out into the street.

He got them out of town and up onto the Interstate without too much trouble. Felicity settled in quietly beside him, apparently trusting him to be as good as his word. Taggart gripped the steering wheel and stared straight ahead.

Soon they'd be taking the highway north, provided he could see it. The snow had already covered the roadway and was still coming down so thick and fast that the signs were all but invisible. The headlights of a semi appeared dimly in the rearview mirror.

Taggart sucked in his breath. It had been in weather like this, the first snow of a heavy storm, that he and Noah had had their accident. A semi had come up behind them fast then, too. His jaw clenched. He felt a cold sweat break out against the back of his neck.

They'd been damned lucky that time. He didn't expect to be that lucky twice.

"Shall I put on the radio and see if I can get the weather station?"

He took a jerky breath. "Yeah, why not?"

Felicity did. Snow, they said in cheerful tones.

"No kidding," Taggart said through his teeth, one eye on the semi. It was getting closer.

High winds, they said. Low visibility. Not a good night to travel. Stay home if you could. Use chains if you were attempting one of the passes.

"We aren't attempting any passes, are we?" Felicity asked.

"No. We shouldn't have any trouble. This is pretty much a straight shot until we get to the hills leading up toward Elmer."

The wind shook the truck, making it harder to steer. The sign for the exit to the highway north loomed suddenly in the swirling whiteness. In his rearview mirror the semi seemed almost on his tail. His whole body tensed.

Then the off ramp was in front of him, he guided the truck onto it, and scant seconds later the semi roared past.

His body sagged suddenly as if all the air had gone out of him.

"Are you all right?" Felicity leaned toward him, her expression worried. "Taggart?"

He straightened and ran his tongue over his lips. "Yeah, of course. I'm ... fine." He loosened his grip on the wheel and found that his hands were shaking.

Felicity wasn't convinced. "Is it the storm? Should we be driving in it? Is it too bad?"

"No," he said, relieved his voice didn't sound as shaky as it felt. "I was just...it was...sort of a déjà vu. The accident..."

"Do you want to stop? Go back?" She reached over and laid a hand on his arm. Her touch felt warm, intimate. The last thing he needed right now. He shifted his arm, and she pulled her hand away.

"No. We'll be fine. It was just...seeing those headlights in the mirror." He drew in a deep, careful breath and let it out slowly. "Really. No problem." He turned and gave her the sort of tough-guy-in-charge smile he gave crowds after he rode a bull.

It must not have worked, because Felicity said, "If you want to stop, we'll stop."

"No."

The miles passed slowly. Taggart kept his eyes on what he hoped was the road, though signs of it were fast disappearing beneath the accumulating snowfall. Felicity sat silently, staring out the windshield. Every once in a while he could feel her turn her gaze on him. He kept his straight ahead. He couldn't go faster because visibility was poor. Even if it hadn't been, they wouldn't have made good time on the snow-covered road.

At least they didn't meet many vehicles heading the other way. A couple of trucks, a few cars. It wasn't a night to be out, that was for sure. The road curved and Taggart took his foot off the gas, slowing without braking.

"Look!" Felicity pointed across the road into the field that sloped off from where the curve in the road began. "There's a car over there!" Through the falling snow, Taggart could just barely make it out.

A car coming the other way had missed the turn. As they got closer, Taggart could see two men behind the vehicle, pushing it, while a third tried to steer it back up out of the ditch onto the road. They weren't getting very far. The car had out-of-state plates. Taggart wasn't surprised.

He let the truck slide slowly to a stop on the shoulder. "Wait here." He shut off the engine, climbed out and crossed the road. "Need a hand?"

It turned out they needed more than a hand. Hunters, out for a week's vacation, they hadn't come prepared for the eventualities of fall in Montana.

"It's October," one of them complained. "My God, you're not supposed to have snow in October!"

"Hardly ever seen anything like it," another said, "and I'm from Illinois. My brothers—" he jerked his head at the other two "—live in Florida."

Figures, Taggart thought. He didn't say anything, just went back for his chains.

"Are they all right?" Felicity asked.

"They will be." Provided he could get them out. He thought with the chains he could. Then, if they drove slow enough and didn't try anything fancy—like using the brakes—they could make it to town. He carried the chains back to the car.

"How do you stand it?" one of the Florida brothers asked, shivering in his boots, while Taggart bent to put on the chains.

"You get used to it." Taggart worked in silence after that, giving directions only when he had to. It was easier to do it himself. Finally, when he had the chains on, he straightened up. The snow stung his cheeks. The wind tugged at his hat and he pulled it back down tight.

"That should do it. You steer," he commanded one. "We'll push." He leaned into the back of the car. In a matter of minutes they had the car back on the road.

They fell all over him saying thank you. Taggart shrugged it off. "Where're you headed?"

"Back to Bozeman when the snow lets up. *If* the snow lets up," one of the Florida brothers added with a sunbelter's scepticism.

"I'd wait till it quits snowing to go over the pass." He might have risked it himself. He knew better than to encourage them to. "You can take the chains."

"But—" The one from Illinois started to argue.

"My folks live in Bozeman. You can drop the chains off with them." Taggart reached inside his jacket and pulled out a pen and one of his business cards. He scrawled his folks' address and phone number on it and handed it over.

"Can't tell you how grateful we are," babbled the Illinois brother.

"Much obliged," agreed both Floridians.

"No problem." To be honest, Taggart had been grateful for the distraction. It was easier putting on chains in a blizzard than sitting next to Felicity in the warm cab of his truck. He stopped now and took a deep breath, gearing himself up for the last few miles. Finally, when the hunters were out of sight, he let out a frosty breath and opened the door to the truck.

It was toasty warm and welcoming, and Felicity was smiling at him. So much for distractions. He sucked in his breath.

"Local hero." She grinned at him.

Taggart knocked the snow off his hat and kicked his boots against the running board. "You got to help each other out when the weather's like this."

"They're lucky you came along."

"I'm a damn fool to be coming along," Taggart said grimly. "I should've paid closer attention this afternoon. I'd never have brought you down for dinner if I'd known."

"I don't mind," she said. "Truly."

I do, Taggart thought.

They moved even more slowly now. Miles he could cover in minutes on clear pavement took more than an hour in weather like this. He was glad Becky was asleep at Noah's. If she weren't, she'd be worrying. The road had completely disappeared by the time they turned onto the county road that led from the highway up into the foothills. Five miles more and they'd reach Elmer. It would feel like fifty before they got there.

Taggart was driving by instinct and feel now. There was no visibility. That was the down side. The up side, he told himself, was that his preoccupation with the storm kept him from thinking so much about Felicity. At least he knew the route like the back of his hand, and he figured that would make the difference.

But just as they came around the bend by the creek, a buck leapt out of the trees in front of him. Instinctively he hit the brakes—and saved the buck. It loped off into the snowstorm and disappeared.

They weren't so lucky.

The truck slewed sideways, then slid down the incline toward the creek.

* * *

"Are you all right?" Taggart's voice was in her ear.

Felicity, who'd banged her head against the door's window as the truck came to a halt, struggled to sit up as straight as she could. "Yes." She was shaken, nothing more. But the truck, she could tell, now sat a steep angle quite a ways down an embankment from the road.

"You're sure?" Taggart was peering at her worriedly, bracing himself against the steering wheel so he wouldn't come sliding into her.

She nodded. "Truly. I'm fine. Are you?" He looked almost white in the light reflected off the snow.

"Okay." He tried to turn and open his door. It wasn't easy due to the angle at which the truck had come to rest.

"I can get mine open," Felicity offered.

"No. You stay here. No sense in you getting any colder." He managed to shove his door open and climb out. Felicity watched him walk around the truck, surveying the damage. She rolled down her window. "Is it bad?"

His mouth twisted. "Depends on what you call bad. The truck's all right."

"But?" she prompted.

He sighed. "But I don't see us getting out of here without the chains I gave our friend from Illinois." He stood, hands on hips, staring at the truck, a grim look on his face. The wind whipped snow into his face, and he turned, hunching his shoulders against its force.

"We can't push it back up?" Felicity knew even as she said the words what the answer would be.

"Nope." He scowled and kicked at the snow with one booted foot. The wind howled. Felicity wanted to roll up the window, but she didn't want him to feel she was deserting him.

"Come back in," she suggested.

"I'll call Noah on the cellular," he said, then cursed under his breath.

"What's wrong?"

"I forgot. I don't have the cellular with me. Damn it." He slapped his hand against the side of the truck, clearly furious with himself.

Not having a cellular herself, nor ever having had occasion to use one, Felicity wasn't as upset as he was. "Don't worry about it," she said.

"I'll walk."

"In this?" The snow had obliterated every landmark. Felicity had no idea where they were. She supposed Taggart did, but the wind was still howling down out of the northwest, making the already-falling temperatures seem even colder. "How far is it?"

"Three, four miles."

"You can't walk that far in this."

"I can," he said stubbornly. And he was a man who'd ridden bulls for a living. Probably he could.

"Maybe," she agreed. "But don't. Please, don't," Felicity repeated. "It's too dangerous."

"I know the road."

"You can't *see* the road."

"I could follow it without seeing it."

"But you might get lost. You might get hurt. You might freeze. I wouldn't have any idea if you were all right or not. And you have to think about Becky."

His eyes met hers. "What about Becky?"

"You said you stopped going down the road because of her. You didn't want to be away from her."

"So?"

"It wasn't just being away, was it? It was because you were afraid something might happen? That maybe you wouldn't be so lucky next time? That maybe Becky wouldn't have a dad if you kept on going?"

She could see by the look in his eyes that she'd hit him right where he lived. He sucked in his breath sharply. His teeth came together. His knuckles went white against the red frame of the truck.

"Don't go," she said.

She didn't know what she was asking of him. To climb back in the cab and sit there—for *hours*—beside her. Keeping his hands to himself. Sharing body heat but not the joy of physical intimacy. He'd die of frustration.

He'd rather die in a blizzard! A younger, more cocksure man would have scoffed at her and gone on his way. A single man with no responsibilities would have gone and to hell with the risk.

But Taggart had been minding his own business, hurrying home for Christmas, and been nailed by a semi. Taggart had seen laughing, joking colleagues—more than one—get on a bull and a minute later or a day later be stone-cold dead. Taggart had a daughter who had only one parent.

He wasn't taking unnecessary risks—not with his life, anyway.

Grimly, he hauled open the door and climbed in. Felicity smiled.

"Roll up your window, for God's sake," he snapped, shoving himself as hard as he could against the driver's-side door, but even gravity was against him, dragging him toward her.

She shot him a quick, nervous look and hastily rolled it up. "Sorry."

"No, I'm sorry." Taggart hunched his shoulders. "I shouldn't have jumped on you. I'm just mad. I should have brought the damn phone. I always bring the damn phone!" But he hadn't this time because he hadn't wanted anyone disturbing his evening with Felicity. He didn't want Becky calling him and checking up on him. He didn't want his folks ringing to see what he was doing for the weekend since they knew he had it free.

Wouldn't they like to know what he was doing? He swallowed a groan.

Felicity huddled in the far corner of the cab. At least she didn't have gravity to fight with. Her legs were tucked up under her and she was sitting with her arms wrapped tightly around her torso, which Taggart could see shivering inside her thin jacket.

Since the engine was off, the heater was off, and because Felicity had opened the window to talk to him, the temperature in the cab had dropped dramatically. He shivered, too.

Felicity opened the blanket she had around her. "I'll share," she offered.

He scrunched back even further against the door. "No," he said. "I'm fine."

And so they sat. Or rather, Felicity huddled and Taggart braced himself, his arm against the steering wheel, his feet pressed into the floor. The wind flung snow against the truck, whipping it furiously, and on the windshield now some of it was beginning to stick, cutting visibility even more. Soon they were in their own little cocoon, just the two of them. Not something Taggart particularly wanted to dwell on.

He shifted, slipped and caught himself. He shoved himself back hard against the door.

Felicity looked at him. He looked at her, then away again.

"How long are you going to keep that up?" she asked him quietly after a moment.

"Keep what up?"

"Fighting the laws of nature." He glanced her way and saw a faint smile light her face. "Gravity, for instance."

He flushed. "You want me to fall on top of you?"

Her cheek dimpled as her smile widened. "It would be warmer."

He stared. Was she suggesting . . . ?

He gave her a hard, searching look. She met it evenly, steadily. God, she was lovely. Even half frozen, teeth chattering, she made his heart kick over.

Which was exactly the problem, wasn't it?

He didn't want his heart kicking over. He wanted to be immune. He didn't want to want what he knew he couldn't have.

If Felicity were just some buckle bunny, like the girls who hung around after the rodeo looking for a cowboy to spend the night with, well, he supposed he could handle that. A roll in a truck cab wasn't exactly his idea of great sex, but he could manage it. But that wasn't what Felicity would want.

Was it?

Oh, God.

He ran his tongue over his lips. "If I stop fighting . . . gravity—" he gave the word a harsh twist "—chances are that won't be the only law of nature I give in to."

There, he couldn't have spelled it out any more clearly than that. He looked at her, brows arched, waiting for some reply.

Felicity took her time. Finally, she nodded. "There is that possibility," she said slowly. Her voice was soft, soothing, almost. But was it a yes or a no?

At least with Julie he'd known that much! When she'd wanted him she was all over him like a case of measles. When she hadn't, she was yelling and chucking things at him, then packing her bags and slamming out the door.

With Julie there had been no *possibilities*.

"We're going to be here all night, aren't we?" Felicity asked him now in that same soft voice.

"Probably." There was a thread of strain in his. He wondered if she could hear it.

She shifted, untucked her hands from between her arms and sides, and held them out to him. "Then come here, Taggart. We'll keep each other warm."

Nine

—

The moment she said the words, she was afraid she had shocked him. She'd shocked herself.

Or maybe, to be honest, she hadn't. Not really. Maybe she just thought she ought to be shocked. It wasn't exactly typical Felicity Albright behavior, practically inviting a man into her arms.

But shocked or not, Felicity wasn't sorry she'd done it.

She had loved Dirk and she had mourned him. She had been two years without ever once feeling desire or even interest in another man. But now she did. She supposed it was perverse that it happened to be Taggart Jones—a man who clearly wanted nothing to do with her—on an emotional level, anyway.

But she knew from loving Dirk that the heart chose to love where the mind often did not. Common sense and so-called "good judgment" had little to do with it. If it had, she'd never have loved Dirk.

Certainly her parents had despaired of her interest in the weedy, gifted boy Dirk had been. Though he could do most anything he set his mind to, his consuming interest in music to the exclusion of almost everything else made him questionable boyfriend material, much less a good prospective husband.

But somehow she and Dirk had been the making of each other. He had taught her to look beyond the confines of their upbringing, to reach for the stars, to strive and work and hope. And she had taught him how to love, how to share a passion, how to engage others' interest even if they weren't as gifted as he. She had given him an anchor in the stormy sea of professional music. She had shown him that he had value as a person beyond how he played the night before. They were good for each other. Perhaps Dirk had suspected it. Felicity certainly had.

She felt the same way about Taggart now.

He was different from Dirk. He wasn't weedy, for one thing. He was hard and lean and muscled. He was dark where Dirk had been blond. He was a talker. Dirk had always let his music speak for him. But deep down he reminded her of Dirk.

He was intense, committed, determined, good at what he did and a gifted teacher, as well. She'd seen the way he could communicate with his students. She'd seen the hero worship in their eyes. She'd seen him earn it—not just with his bull riding, but with the concern and the vision he shared with each of the students who came to one of his schools. She knew he wasn't only preparing them to ride bulls. He was giving them the keys to a successful life. He was a man who inspired trust.

Felicity trusted him.

Probably, she acknowledged, more than he trusted himself. And she needed him—and not just to keep her warm tonight.

She needed him to warm her soul. And she dared to think he needed her, as well. Whatever had happened to Taggart because of his marriage, she had heard enough now to know that it hadn't been good. But that didn't mean marriage couldn't be good. She prayed he would give her a chance to teach him that.

He didn't move quickly. There was no eagerness. She could see the wariness, the strain in his face. The skin over his cheekbones was taut, the green eyes probing, looking for—what?

Love? She didn't think so. Not yet. Not more than the physical kind, at least. She knew well enough that he wanted that, but in the cab of a truck...?

"Trade me places," Taggart's voice had a slightly ragged edge to it.

Felicity slid forward, and he moved along the seat behind her until he was pressed against the passenger side door. Then he wrapped his arms around her, drawing her against him so that she was practically sitting in his lap. She snuggled back, pressing into his warmth. It felt so good. Not only the warmth, but the holding. It had been so long since she'd been in a man's arms.

But it wasn't just that, either. It was the man. Taggart. Taggart holding her. Taggart's breath against the back of her neck. Taggart's hands tucking themselves around, cupping her breasts. She could feel his fingers through the jacket she wore. His thighs were warm and hard beneath her bottom. She shifted, settling in more completely, her body molding itself to his. Shifting again, wriggling. Accommodating.

Taggart's arms tightened. She heard a swift intake of breath.

"What's the matter?"

"Nothing." There was a faintly strangled sound to his tone.

She twisted clear around on his lap to look at him. "You can't tell me you're all right," she said. "When we slid into the ditch... were you hurt?"

A muscle ticked in his jaw. His mouth was only bare inches from hers. So close she could feel the warmth of his breath when he spoke. "No."

"Then—"

He shifted then, too, shrugging against the seat as if to ease some discomfort, and suddenly she understood—and felt her cheeks burn. "Oh."

Taggart grimaced. "Yes. Oh," he echoed, his tone now ruefully self-mocking. "Sorry. I told you—those laws of nature."

"Do you want me to move off?"

But when she tried, he held her fast. "Do you want to stay warm or not?"

"Yes, but—"

He shifted her sideways slightly, so that her feet rested on the other end of the bench seat and her bottom pressed firmly into him. Then his arms tightened again. "Tell me some more about your trip to Europe."

She knew he was making small talk, but she obliged him. She talked—haltingly at first, but then with more ease, describing the hostel she and Dirk had stayed in near Lake Como. She told him about their visit to Venice.

"Did you ride in a gondola?" He sounded almost jealous.

She shook her head. "Too expensive. We took the vaporetto. Water bus," she explained. "We saw the same things—and just as romantically, really. The romance is within, I think."

"Yeah." His breath caressed her ear, making her shiver, and all her small talk went for naught. She was intensely aware of him again.

"Your turn," she said. "Tell me about . . . about . . ."

"Cheyenne? Reno? The Cow Palace? All those romantic spots?"

"Why not? I haven't been any of those places."

So he told her. About the places, about the people—and the bulls—he'd seen. It sounded fun and grueling and exciting and tiring. "Do you miss it?" she asked, turning her head to get a glimpse of his face. "The traveling?"

He looked thoughtful. "Some. Now and then. It gets in your blood, I guess. But I knew I couldn't do it forever. And with Becky I just had to quit a little sooner than I might have otherwise. I don't regret it, if that's what you mean."

He didn't sound like a man who had many regrets—besides his marriage. She wanted to ask about it and wondered if she dared. The wind rocked the truck again, and Felicity felt Taggart's arms tighten around her.

"Did your . . . wife travel with you?" she ventured finally.

"Once." His voice was flat. "She didn't like it."

"I'm sorry," Felicity apologized for asking. "It's none of my business."

"It's history," Taggart said. "Not very pretty history, so I don't talk about it much. We were two people in the throes of lust. We should have seen it for what it was. I do now. I won't make the same mistake again."

There was nothing to say after that. The snow buried them deeper. Felicity tried to imagine a woman who could only feel lust for Taggart Jones. It was so much less than she felt herself. She settled back more deeply into the warmth of his embrace. He shifted beneath her.

"Sorry," she muttered again.

"A little torture never hurt a guy."

She smiled. "I didn't know you were a masochist."

"I ride bulls, don't I?" He was smiling, too, but Felicity had seen the danger.

"Don't you . . . get scared sometimes?"

"If you concentrate on the fear, you might as well not do it. The fear is more likely to kill you than the bull. I'm not saying a bull can't kill. Some of the best riders have died in the arena. If it's your time, it's your time, I guess. But you can make it your time, if you panic. When you ride a bull, you have to trust your instincts and all that practice you did. It's just—you're there, the bull's there. Are you going to ride or not? If you are, you can't think. You just have to react."

Felicity listened and understood. She felt like that herself. She was here. Taggart was here. She'd spent two years thinking. Hibernating.

Now she just had to react.

She kissed him. She couldn't help it. She was sitting on his lap, snuggled in his arms, her lips bare inches—ten centimeters, she would have told her kids when they did the metric system—from his. The temptation was too great.

She had kissed him before and regretted it. She didn't regret it now.

Perhaps because he didn't seem stunned, only eager, as if the fires, long banked, had suddenly burst into full flame and he was as desperate for her touch as she was for his.

The first kiss had lasted less than a second. This one went on and on.

Lips only at first, then tongues, tasting, teasing. Teeth nibbling, nipping. Mouths that hungered, that sipped and savored. Until just the touch of their mouths wasn't enough anymore. Felicity rubbed her cheek against his, loving the soft-rough feel of the day's growth of whiskers. Men's skin was so different from women's. She lifted a hand and smoothed it along his jaw, traced the curve of his ear. Her fingers crept up to ease his hat off and stroke his hair.

Dirk's hair had been long enough to thread her fingers through. Taggart's was short, clipped close to the back of his head, trimmed above his ears. Long enough on top, though, to tousle. Felicity tousled it. She played in it, running her fingers over his scalp, brushing, combing, loving the soft silky feel of it.

She felt his hands burrow in her hair, too. Not only his hands. His face. He pressed his lips to her ear, nuzzled her with his nose. And all the while, his hands wove themselves in and out, smoothing and teasing, raking and caressing. The simple feel of his fingers was so wonderful that she felt a shiver run right down her spine.

"Not warm enough yet?" Taggart said. The ragged edge was still there, but she could hear a smile in his tone.

"Warm," she murmured against his cheek. "Very warm. How about you?"

"Hot. And you know it." She felt his jaw tighten and felt a moment's qualm. She didn't want to tease. She wanted to love. She kissed him again, tenderly at first, trying to set him at ease, to let him know how she felt. The response she got moved from tenderness to urgency in seconds. His tongue slipped between her lips, plunging into the heat of her mouth, delving, seeking. And Felicity met it with an urgency of her own. This, too, was a part of love, and if this was what he wanted . . .

She twisted further to come around to hold him. He moaned, his hips lifting to press against her bottom. She felt the heat of his arousal right through her wool trousers and his jeans. She eased away from him slightly and reached between them, her fingers finding the buckle of his belt.

He stilled suddenly, sucked in his breath. "Felicity." His eyes met hers, dark and desperate.

"I can help."

He gave a shaky half laugh. "I know you can. But—" he shook his head and let out a ragged sigh "—you shouldn't."

"No?" She should have been embarrassed at her wanton behavior. He was the father of one of her pupils, for goodness' sake. He could easily get her fired.

He wouldn't. She didn't know how she knew that, but she did. Taggart would never do anything to hurt her. She looked into his eyes.

"No, Taggart?" Her breath was a whisper against his mouth.

He shut his eyes and dragged in a ragged breath. "Isn't the shoe supposed to be on the other foot?" he asked, a tremor in his voice. He sounded halfway between pain and amusement.

"You mean, aren't you supposed to be seducing me?"

He opened his eyes to meet hers again. "Something like that."

She smiled. "Go ahead."

He groaned. Then his hands, which had been still against her back, very slowly began to move, coming forward, sliding along her rib cage, thumbs inward as they came up beneath her jacket and, through her sweater, cupped her breasts, then stroked across them, the pads of his thumbs caressing her nipples, making her shiver. She bit her lip. She saw him smile.

She bent her head, laying her forehead against his temple, letting her hair brush across his chin, his lips, his cheek. With her tongue she touched the curve of his ear. A shudder ran through him. She could feel it.

He shifted, and suddenly she had more access to his belt. She didn't have a lot of experience with world championship belt buckles, but she couldn't think of a better time to get some. She fumbled with it, then fumbled some more, muttering and feeling a heat climb into her cheeks that had as much to do with embarrassment at her ineptitude as it did with arousal.

For the moment, anyway. But then the hook gave, the belt opened beneath her fingers, and her hand lay against the soft denim covering him.

His hands stilled against her breasts, each of her nipples caught between a thumb and forefinger. Slowly, carefully, not fumbling this time, Felicity undid the button and lowered his zipper, then slid her hand inside and touched him.

He sucked in a sharp breath. His thumbs and fingers drew on her nipples, sending a shaft of desire straight to the core of her. Felicity's fingers tightened around him, moving slowly against the rigid column of his flesh. He trembled. He pressed his head back hard against the window. His whole body stiffened.

"Felisssssity!" Her name came out on a hiss of urgency. Taggart's hips surged, and then he shuddered and sank back down in the seat, his eyes closed, his jaw locked. Felicity pressed her lips against his cheek.

He quivered and let out a groan.

"Taggart?" She felt suddenly awkward, embarrassed. She didn't want to pull her hand away, not yet, but if she left it . . .

"God. I'm . . . sorry. I've never—" He pulled one of his hands away from her and pressed it against his eyes. "Hell."

"It's . . . all right." She hated the tremble in her voice. She wanted to sound calm, blasé, a woman of the world.

He made a ragged sound deep in his throat. "Yeah, sure." He opened his eyes and looked at her ruefully. "I should never have let you touch me. It's . . . it's been a long time. Too long, obviously." His gaze slid away. "It's no excuse, but—"

"It's a good excuse," she said softly. "The best."

He looked at her. "But—"

"I wouldn't like to think I'm just the next in a long line of women."

He straightened. His brows drew down. "You're not."

She leaned forward and touched his cheek with her lips. "I'm glad."

"Yeah, well, I could've just told you. I didn't have to . . . to demonstrate." He gave her a rueful look.

Felicity smiled. "Did you really think we were going to be able to make love in here?" Her gaze moved doubtfully around the narrow confines of the truck cab, then came back to him.

Taggart sighed. "I wasn't doing much thinking, if you want to know the truth." He leaned his forehead against hers, then reached down to adjust his jeans.

Felicity eased her hand away, but she didn't want to stop touching him entirely, so she slid her hand beneath his shirt to curve her fingers over his rib cage. Taggart zipped his jeans again and settled back against the door. Then, after a moment's hesitation, he slipped his arms around Felicity and drew her close.

She sighed, resting her head on his shoulder, settling in. Loving the closeness. Loving him.

She wasn't sure precisely when she realized this was love she was feeling. Maybe it was when she watched him teach the cowboys how to ride bulls. Maybe it was when she saw him ride one of his own. Maybe it was when he took her to dinner to tell her about Sam's parents even when he obviously didn't want to get involved. Maybe it was when he let her touch him, feel close to him, *give to him*. It didn't matter. It was enough that she knew. It was enough that she did. She sighed and turned her head into the curve of his neck and shoulder.

"Are you...all right?" Taggart asked worriedly. "If you...I mean, I'd like...if you want..." His voice trailed off, a note of chagrin lingering.

She touched her lips to the warm, slightly stubbly skin on his jaw. "It's fine. I'm fine. Better than fine. I haven't been so right in a very long time."

Go figure, Taggart thought.

A guy makes a fool of himself, behaves with all the savoir faire of a high school kid on his first hot date, and a girl acts like he's done good, like she's pleased with him!

Not all girls, he reminded himself. This girl.

Woman, he corrected himself. Holding her, sharing the warmth of her body as it pressed into his, reflecting on her words—her generosity—he knew she was no child. She was certainly nothing like Julie had been. He could just imagine what Julie would have said about what had just happened! It wouldn't have been complimentary, that was for sure.

"Taggart?"

"Hmm?" He lifted his hand and stroked her hair. She sighed and snuggled closer. The truck shuddered, buffeted by another gust of wind.

"Tell me about going down the road."

"Nothin' to tell. A whole lot of miles in trucks and cars. A little bit of being jerked around on the back of this bull and that bull."

"There's more to it than that."

Not according to Julie. But he shifted, settling Felicity more comfortably on his lap, and said, "Well, yeah, I guess."

She lifted her head, brushing her hair away from her face, turning so that her nose brushed against his cheek. "So tell me. Why do you love it? You must or you wouldn't do it."

He shrugged, feeling self-conscious. "It's hard to explain."

She drew a line along his jaw. "You explained lots of things to those cowboys in your school."

He shook his head. "Not the same thing." But she was looking at him expectantly, and he knew she wasn't going to let him off the hook.

"It's a challenge," he said slowly. "It's taking all you are—all your courage and your know-how and your desire—and putting them all on the line. It's focusing all your attention on one moment in time, demanding everything you've got. It's a risk. It's skill. It's—let's face it—partly luck. It's life. Life is skill and courage and know-how and desire—and luck—all rolled into one." He stared into the fogged-over, snow-covered windshield, trying to explain the sensation, the emotion, the essence of what those years of miles and seconds of rides had meant to him. "It's a distillation of what it means to do your best, to live your life to the fullest. Sometimes you win. Sometimes you lose. But you always try."

He turned his head back to look at her. The expression on her face, the way she was looking at him, made the heat crawl into his face. He gave an awkward shrug. "See, I told you I couldn't explain it. I'm no philosopher."

"I wouldn't trade you for Aristotle." Her finger traced once more along his jawline, then she threaded her fingers in his hair, leaned over, and, with exquisite gentleness, she kissed him. She kissed him first on the forehead, then on each of his eyelids, then the tip of his nose, and, finally—he thought he'd die waiting for her—on his mouth.

It was a tender kiss, a gentle kiss, and yet it spoke of hunger and yearning and a million things that Taggart knew were out there somewhere out of reach—both his and hers.

If it weren't for Julie, he thought, the ache inside him growing, billowing, filling every inch of his being... If he hadn't failed so miserably once, he thought as need seared him... Not sexual need; no, it was more than that. It was emotional need, personal need. The desire to share, to be part of something larger, to connect. To love.

He shut his eyes tightly. Inside his head he heard the word drumming over and over: If...if...if...

Finally, slowly, he drew back and forced himself to look at her squarely. "Tell me," he said, "more about Dirk."

It was the hardest thing he'd ever done.

* * *

They awoke to the sound of banging on the window of the truck.

Felicity groaned and stretched, stiff from the cold and from being cramped on Taggart's lap. She cracked open one eye. Someone was brushing snow off the glass. Embarrassed to have whoever it might be catch her in Taggart's arms, she hauled herself up, then struggled to push open the driver's side door. Through the cleared glass the early morning sunlight streamed in.

"S'at?" Taggart muttered. He was moving stiffly, too. Barely awake. Felicity didn't know how long they'd finally slept.

She fumbled with the door handle and felt it jerk out of her hand as the door opened and Noah peered in at them.

"Thank God. You all right?"

Felicity straightened and managed a smile, trying to run a hand through her mussed hair. She doubted it was helping. "We're fine," she said. Taggart didn't say anything. She could feel him moving behind her. "Taggart braked to miss a deer," she went on quickly, "and we went off the road."

"So I see. No chains?" Noah looked over her at his buddy, an expression of disapproval on his face.

"He lent them to some hunters who went off the road below Clyde Park." Felicity gave Noah a bright smile and eased herself toward him, blocking his view of Taggart who was, she hoped—judging from the movements behind her—buckling his belt.

"You're out early," Taggart said gruffly now. He edged around and opened the passenger side door—belt buckled, Felicity was glad to see—and stepped down into a foot of snow.

"Becky was worried."

Taggart ducked his head. "You told her I was all right, didn't you?"

"I told her I figured you'd decided to sit out the storm somewhere. I didn't know you were all right." Noah gave him an accusing look. "I wasn't saying something I had to go back on. You could have rung up."

"Forgot to take the cellular with me." Taggart tugged his hat down on his head and met Noah's gaze defiantly.

Noah's brows lifted. "Forgot?"

"Forgot."

Felicity felt as though she was watching a duel—glares at ten paces. "You've been known to forget things at times," he reminded Noah pointedly.

Neither spoke for a long moment. Then Noah kicked one of the tires. "Yeah, I reckon so." The staring contest went on for a few more moments, then Noah cocked his head Felicity's way. "You kept him in line, I hope." He gave her a wink that made her blush furiously. She hoped he'd think her heightened color was due to the still icy wind.

"Of course," she said in her best schoolteacher voice. "He was a perfect gentleman."

Noah laughed. "A perfect gentleman. Whoa! Wait'll I tell Mace and Jed!"

"Stow it," Taggart said gruffly. His face was red, too, and Felicity knew very well it wasn't just from the cold. "Did you come to harass us or are you gonna help get us out of here?"

Noah grinned and headed back to his own truck for chains. But even with the chains they were so far down the slope and at such an angle that they couldn't get out.

"Want me to call a tow truck?" Noah asked.

"No!" Taggart was adamant. "You think Felicity wants the world to know she spent the night in the truck with me?"

Felicity didn't actually care what the world knew, though she realized that was, perhaps, foolish of her. After yesterday evening's display on Apple Street, she knew this was a small town and not anonymous Southern California. "I don't mind."

"You do," Taggart said firmly. He looked her straight in the eye. "Sam Bacon's dad drives the tow truck."

"Oh."

Noah must have got the point, too, for he said, "I'll call Jed," and climbed the slope to his own truck to get his cellular phone.

"Tuck's uncle," Taggart told her. "He won't say a word."

Felicity could well believe that. "Fine."

While they were waiting for Jed, Noah called Tess and told her to get Becky. Then he handed the phone to Taggart.

"Hey, Pard. How you doin'?" There was a tenderness in his voice as he talked to his daughter that melted Felicity's heart. His smile broadened at the sound of her voice, then faded. "I know," he said after a moment. "I know I should've taken it with me. Then I could have called and you wouldn't have worried. I'm sorry."

Taggart's gaze flicked up to meet Felicity's. "She's fine, too." He hesitated, his eyes locking on Felicity's. "Yeah," he said a little hoarsely. "I . . . took good care of her." He looked away, his voice dropping. "Not long now. Jed's coming. I'll see you pretty soon. Promise." He smiled once more. "Love you, too, Pard."

Jed arrived an hour later in a heavy-duty truck with a winch on the back. For cattle as much as machinery, Noah told her.

Felicity smiled at Jed uncertainly, wondering if he, like Orrin Bacon, might look at her and Taggart with speculation in his eyes, but she could barely see them, shadowed as they were beneath the brim of his hat.

He gave her a faint nod, touched a finger to the brim of his hat and followed Noah and Taggart to study the lay of the land. In the end, it took forty-five minutes to get Taggart's truck out. Noah and Taggart discussed and theorized. Jed waited till they were done, then set to work. When they were once more on the road, he rolled down his window, touched his hat brim to her once more, then drove off.

"Talkative, isn't he," she said to Taggart when both Jed and Noah were gone.

Taggart shrugged. "That's Jed."

Once they got back on the road she could see that more than a foot of unseasonable snow blanketed the entire valley. The wind, still blowing, rearranged it in drifts. But the sun was strong and warm.

"It'll melt in two days or less," Taggart said as he drove her up Apple Street. Felicity was suddenly conscious of window curtains on either side. Was one twitching back just a bit? Was another being adjusted just now? She didn't care.

"Good. But I must say, I'm glad it happened." She turned to him and smiled.

He didn't. He looked grave as he parked in front of her house. She started to open the door, but he stopped her. "I'll carry you in."

"I thought you were worried about the neighbors."

His scowl surprised her. "You're right. Is your house un-
locked? I'll go get you some better shoes." He came back a few
minutes later with a pair of deck shoes. "If this is the best you
can do, you'd better go to Bozeman and get prepared for winter."

Felicity slipped them on. "I will. I thought I'd have more
time." She slid down out of the truck and followed him, step-
ping in his footsteps all the way to the door. "Will you come
in?"

"Gotta pick up Becky." But he didn't immediately turn to
go. He ducked his head, staring at the toe of his boot as he
scuffed it through the snow on the porch. "I'm sorry... about
last night. About getting stuck in the snow. About—" his color
deepened "—everything."

"I'm not." She wanted to kiss him. She wanted to take that
look of misery off his face and make him smile the way she
knew he could smile.

She wanted to tell him she loved him. But if the rest of Elmer was ready and waiting to hear it, Taggart wasn't. Not yet.

Felicity wasn't positive that the residents of Apple Street were
aware she had spent the night with Taggart Jones in his truck.
If they were, they were discreet enough not to mention it—at
least in her hearing. And if they passed on that little tidbit to
anyone else, no one told Felicity. But even so, it took her three
days to breathe a sigh of relief.

At last, though, when Monday's classes came and went and
no one pointed a finger in her direction and tittered and giggled, she felt she had weathered the storm.

That storm. And the snowstorm which, as Taggart predicted, had all but melted away by Monday afternoon. In fact,
the weather was almost balmy, making her feel that Friday
night's experience might have been no more than a dream.

But another storm—also one Taggart had predicted—blew
in Monday afternoon.

She had just settled down at her desk to go over some arithmetic assignments when a shadow from the doorway fell across
the floor. She felt a leap in her heart—then she looked up and
discovered it wasn't Taggart, but a man she didn't know.

He wasn't quite as tall as Taggart and not nearly as handsome. In fact, his features reminded Felicity of the pug dog that lived next door to her parents' home in Iowa.

She stood up. "Can I help you?"

"You're Ms. Albright?" His tone reminded her of the pug, too. There was a yappy belligerence in it that made her stay where she was, rather than go around the desk to shake his hand.

She nodded. "That's right. And you are . . . ?"

"Orrin Bacon."

Felicity rubbed her palms surreptitiously against the sides of her skirt, drying them before offering her hand to Sam's father. "How nice of you to drop by. We missed you on Friday. I have the video if you'd like to—"

"Wouldn't," he said. "No time for foolishness." He gave her hand a quick, perfunctory shake. "It's what I came to talk to you about, Ms. Albright. That foolishness you had those kids doin' on Friday. Friday, hell—I mean, heck! They been doin' it for weeks! Waste of time."

"I don't consider it foolishness, Mr. Bacon. Or a waste of time. It's simply another teaching method. One you may not be used to."

"You can say that again! Stupid method. Playing when they oughta be learning." He scowled at her.

Felicity tried not to scowl at him. She drew a careful breath, reminding herself that she wasn't going to win any converts by battle. "Children learn in different ways, Mr. Bacon."

"Nothin' wrong with the way I learned."

"I'm sure there wasn't," Felicity said in as conciliatory a tone as she could manage. "And perhaps you learned well that way."

"So can Sam if you stop coddling him."

"I am not 'coddling' him, Mr. Bacon. Sam is working very hard."

"Making toy guns." He snorted, nostrils flaring. "What the hell for?"

"So he gets a feel for the work that goes into making something. So that he has something to do with his hands while he listens to the tapes I've made of the history."

Another snort. "Tapes! Why can't he just read the book and learn it?"

"He can," Felicity said. "But he hates it. It's a struggle."

"It's work," Orrin Bacon agreed. "Nothin' wrong with work."

"No. But there's nothing wrong with enjoying your work, either."

He looked at her suspiciously, about to argue, then hesitating.

"Do you enjoy your work, Mr. Bacon?"

"Of course. Wouldn't do it if I didn't."

Felicity smiled. "I suspect Sam feels the same way."

"He's got to do it. He's a kid."

And where, Felicity wondered, was the logic in that? Kids shouldn't enjoy life; only adults had that right? "We all have to do things we don't like at times, Mr. Bacon," she agreed. "But when we can learn by doing something that feels right to us, don't you think it's better?"

Bacon clamped his jaw together, not speaking. The look he gave her was wary, suspicious.

"It's just that things are new," she said quietly.

They stared at each other. Bacon looked away first, and Felicity heard him mutter something under his breath about "furriners."

"I beg your pardon?"

His jaw jutted. "I said, I don't like all you hippy foreigners comin' in here tellin' us what to do. Go back to California where you're from."

"I'm from Iowa, Mr. Bacon," she told him. "I only lived in California. But some of my best friends are Californians." She smiled. He didn't. "Look, what it comes down to as far as I'm concerned, is, *is Sam learning?* And I think he is."

Bacon scowled. "You didn't learn that way, I bet."

"No, but I wish I had. I would," she said now, "if I was trying to learn something new."

"You're not a student now. You're a teacher."

"I still can learn. Can you?"

His eyes bugged at her direct challenge. "What? Of course I can. What are you playing at, Ms. Albright?"

"How about a deal?" She was making it up as she went along. "If I can learn something new, something hard, something that I would find challenging, you'll learn something, too?"

"What something?" Orrin Bacon asked suspiciously.

"To let me teach Sam my way."

He pondered that. "What are you going to learn?"

"I don't know yet. Something local. Quilting?" Alice could teach her that. "How to use Uncle Fred's printing press?" She'd love to do that. They could have a class newspaper. "What do you say, Mr. Bacon?"

For a full minute he didn't say anything. Then, at last, he nodded slowly. "But if you don't learn, then you start teaching Sam my way, right?"

"Right."

Orrin Bacon nodded. "All right, Ms. Albright. You got yourself a deal."

Ten

He owed her. Big time. But it was a debt Taggart wasn't at all reluctant to pay. Hell, if the truth were known, he'd been looking forward to it all week!

He was just glad he didn't have a school this weekend that would tie up all his time. Noah had a bunch of bronc riders in, and he would have to show up to do the videotaping, but other than that, he had no commitments.

Except making love to Felicity Albright.

When his parents had called to ask if Becky could come down and spend the weekend with them, well, it wasn't too hard to say yes.

"You won't be lonely, will you?" Becky asked worriedly Friday afternoon when her grandfather came to pick her up.

"I'll survive."

"You can go see Ms. Albright." Becky hadn't said too much about last Friday night. She knew he'd spent it stuck in his truck with Felicity Albright. Undoubtedly she had her own ideas of what transpired. Taggart was quite sure he was better off not knowing what they were.

"I could," he said vaguely. He wasn't going to deny it. Going to see her—making love to her—didn't mean he was going to marry her. Marriage wasn't an option, and he'd told her that. But a little loving—or a lot of loving—in a bed this time, would suit him just fine.

"I knew it!" Becky crowed.

Taggart scowled and pointed a finger at her. "You don't know nothin', young lady."

"I know that's a double negative!" She leapt, giggling, into his arms to kiss him goodbye.

Even though he fully intended to enjoy every moment of his weekend with Felicity Albright, he still felt a little nervous when he knocked on her front door an hour later. He hadn't called her all week—unsure, under the circumstances, what to say.

Now he didn't know, either. And he didn't know what she'd say to him.

The door opened. Her face lit up. "Taggart!"

"I brought dinner," he said, juggling the two small grocery sacks in his arms. "I hope you don't mind." It suddenly occurred to him that she might be going out. He stared at her, stricken.

But she only opened the door wider and smiled a welcome. "Come in."

She didn't step back, so he practically brushed against her as he passed. Certainly he was close enough to catch a whiff of lilacs again. He remembered it from last weekend when he'd held her in his arms, buried his face in her hair. A shaft of pure longing shot through him.

"What have you brought?" She followed him into the kitchen and watched as he unloaded the bags.

"Steak. Potatoes. Lettuce. Tomatoes. A bottle of salad dressing. Ice cream." He brandished each in turn. "Nothing fancy. I just—" He stopped, looking at her. God, she was beautiful. "I've been thinking about you all week," he said. *About touching you again. Loving you. Finishing what we'd only just begun.*

She dimpled. "And I've been thinking about you."

"You... don't have plans? I know I should've called first, but—" he shrugged "—I thought you might say no."

"No, I don't have plans?"

"No, you don't want to see me." He swallowed as their eyes locked.

"I want to see you, Taggart." Her voice was quiet, but firm. Her gaze seemed almost to devour him. "All week I've wanted to see you."

Me, too. He didn't say it, just sucked in a ragged breath. "Good." He cleared his throat. "That's good."

Still they stared at each other. Needing. Wanting. Hungering. And not for steak and potatoes. But since they were the excuse, Taggart felt obliged to try to get through them first.

"Do you want to do them on the grill?" Felicity asked him, unwrapping the meat.

"We can broil them."

"The grill would do a better job."

"But then we'd have to be outside." A grin quirked the corner of his mouth. "And Cloribel and company would be supervising."

"They'll know you're here, anyway," Felicity said. "They'll see your truck."

He shook his head. "I parked on Main Street," Taggart said. "In front of the bar."

"And you don't think they saw you coming up the street?"

"Maybe. But they won't think I'm still here hours from now."

"Are you going to be here hours from now?" she asked, raising her eyebrows. She leaned against one of the kitchen cabinets and crossed her arms over her breasts.

"I'd like to be."

A flush crept up Felicity's cheeks. She hugged herself tightly. She reminded Taggart of a doe, cornered, looking for a way to bolt. But then something inside her seemed to settle. She dropped her arms so that they hung loose at her sides. She pushed herself away from the counter and lifted her face to his.

"Good," she said.

It was all he needed. In two steps he was across the room and taking her in his arms. He folded her against him, kissing her with a week's—hell, months'!—worth of longing. The night they had spent in the truck had given him a brief, incomplete satisfaction. If for a few minutes his body had been sated, the rest of him had only grown to hunger for her more and more.

He needed her in every way he could think of. Mostly he needed to give her the loving she'd already given him. "I want you," he murmured against her lips. "I want to love you, Felicity."

She pulled back just far enough to look up at him with doe-like eyes. "Yes," she whispered. "Oh, yes."

She took his hand and led him up the stairs into her bedroom. The furniture was old and heavy, dark and decidedly masculine. Fred's, no doubt. But the walls were cream-colored, and airy Irish lace curtains brought a contrasting feminine lightness to the room. Seascape watercolors hung on the walls, and on the table by her bed Taggart saw the photograph of a smiling young man. He tensed, knowing it was Dirk.

Felicity felt his tension and saw where he was looking. She reached over and picked up the photo, handing it to him. Taggart forced himself to look. Dirk was a combination of determination and gentleness. A kind man, Taggart thought. The sort of man Felicity deserved.

"He made you happy," he said, forcing the words through his too-tight throat.

Felicity brushed her fingers over Dirk's picture. "Yes," she said, And then she took it from his nerveless fingers and put it in her dresser drawer. Then she looped her hands around his neck and tugged his face down to hers. "And so will you."

He would, Taggart vowed, shutting his eyes. Or die trying. At least for tonight.

He threaded his fingers in her hair, luxuriating in the heavy silken tresses as he weighed them in his hands. He kissed her again. First her nose, then her eyes, then her mouth. He feathered kisses along her jaw and nuzzled her neck. Felicity made a sound almost like a purr.

He opened his eyes and smiled at her, then sat on the bed, drawing her into his arms. She came willingly. Eagerly. But there was a reserve about her, too. He had her. But he didn't have all of her. Yet.

His hands roved over her—arms, shoulders, breasts, hips. Learning her curves and contours. He remembered doing things like this to Felicity in his dreams and waking, hot and hungry and eminently unsatisfied. The reality was far better.

Now, smiling, he skimmed her scoop-necked shirt up and over her head in one quick movement and tossed it aside. And there she was, before him, creamy pale skin, narrow bones and a peach-colored bra that barely covered the fullness of her breasts. He cupped them in his hands, brushed his thumbs over them, making her tremble at his touch.

She reached for him, then, fingers fumbling with the front of his shirt.

"They're snaps," Taggart said. "Not buttons."

She laughed a little unsteadily. "You'd think I could see that." She undid them carefully, one by one, until his chest was exposed, and she ran her hands over it—over him—and it was his turn to tremble.

He lay back and she came with him, settling alongside him so that they lay knee to knee, nose to nose. They kissed, nipped, nibbled. He reached around and undid the clasp of her bra, then eased it off, and let the soft weight of her breasts spill into his hands. Then he bent his head and touched them each in turn with his tongue.

"Taggart!" Felicity wriggled against him, hooking an ankle over his calf and pressing against him.

"Mmm?" He didn't raise his head, but his hands kept working—though it didn't seem much like work, this caressing, touching, undoing the fastener of her slacks and sliding the zipper down. With care he hooked his thumbs in the waistband and eased them down over her hips, past her bottom. He did pull away long enough to tug them off and send them following the top she'd worn. And then he looked back at Felicity as she lay on the bed beside him.

She was everything a man could ask for. Warm and willing. Eager and waiting. Just for him.

She smiled and held out her arms to him. He shucked his boots and jeans and briefs, skinned off the scrap of peach-colored lace that was the last thing Felicity wore, and then he settled between her legs, trembling with anticipation.

Slow, he told himself. *Take it slow.* There might have been an excuse for last time. There was none now. This time was for her. For both of them.

It was a dance of touch and taste. His fingers and hers. His lips and hers. Gentle brushing. Soft nibbling. Here. There. Everywhere. Circles and spirals, loops and lines. Focusing. Centering. Closer. Closer.

"Now," Felicity whispered. And she took him in. Loved him. Let him love her. The world splintered around them, and reality—and Felicity—brought him the satisfaction that dreams never had.

It was everything he wanted. It was more than he'd hoped. It was everything he feared. It was more than he dared.

He'd sought this once and thought he'd found it with Julie. He'd been wrong. Dead wrong. He'd consoled himself after she'd left him, telling himself it didn't matter because such joy didn't exist. For eight years he'd believed that.

Wrong again.

Eyes shut, he lay perfectly still. Felicity's fingers were gripping him hard, holding him close.

"I love you," she whispered.

Taggart felt his insides knot. Love you. Love you. The words echoed in his head. They were so easily spoken. So lightly said. Julie had said them. Then he'd believed. In the words. In Julie.

In himself.

And now?

Felicity isn't Julie, he told himself. But Felicity wasn't the problem. The problem, as Julie had been all too quick to point out, was him. A tight, painful sound filled the back of his throat.

Felicity's fingers stroked his back. Her lips teased the curve of his ear. "Taggart?" she said. Her breath tickled his cheek.

He opened his eyes and slowly, very slowly, eased himself away from her, bracing above her on his hands, looking down into her face. She was smiling. An angel's smile. Something else he wasn't sure he believed in.

"Don't," he said, looking away, rolling off.

Her smile faded. "Don't? Don't what?"

"Don't love me." He shook his head, then turned his head to look over at her, to try to meet her gaze. It wasn't easy. She looked wounded. Eyes wide, hurt. No surprise. He was good at wounding people. The knowledge stiffened his faltering resolve.

"I don't want love," he told her raggedly.

Felicity didn't reply. She turned onto her side to face him, her expression serious, and she studied him with her big, wide eyes. She was close enough that he could feel her breath touch his cheek, but she didn't touch him.

"What *do* you want?" she asked slowly, almost gently.

He struggled to come up with the words. "Just...what we had. Closeness. A few hours— A little—" He broke off, unable to form them. It sounded crass when he tried to put it into words.

"A little sex?"

He scowled. "That's crude."

"You're the one who is saying it has nothing to do with love!" There was pain in her voice now, and the very sound of it hurt him, too.

Taggart moved away and sat on the side of the bed. "Hell." He rubbed his hands through his hair, then dragged them down his face. "I didn't want this. I never meant—I should never have come."

Felicity sat up, too, shoving herself against the headboard, grabbing the blanket and pulling it around her. "No, you shouldn't have! Not if that's all you're here for. What was tonight, Taggart? Payback time? A return engagement to make up for whatever inadequacies you thought you displayed last weekend in the truck?"

Her words knifed him. He felt the color rise in his cheeks. He didn't answer. He didn't have to. His silence was condemnation enough.

Felicity made a strangled sound and leapt off the bed. "Well, thank you very much. Consider us even, then, won't you? Now, get dressed and get the hell out!" She was scooping up his jeans and shirt and throwing them at him as she spoke.

He caught them. His boots came sailing, too, one after the other. He caught the first. The second narrowly missed his head. "I didn't mean—I never intended—!" But once more he couldn't find the right words.

"No," Felicity said bitterly. "I can see that now. You never intended anything more than a roll in the sack, did you? Well, you got it. I trust you will keep the news of it to yourself," she said, her lips twisting as she spoke. "Not only would it not do my professional reputation any good, it will prove better than anything that I'm a fool!"

She turned then and darted from the room. Taggart stared after her, feeling like he'd been gored. He heard the door to the bathroom slam. He stood irresolute, for a long moment, wanting to go after her, wanting to tell her it was all a mistake, wanting to say that he loved her, wanted to marry her and live happily ever after.

But this was reality. He got up and started to dress.

She hadn't come out by the time he'd finished. He hesitated outside the bathroom door, then tapped lightly. "Felicity?"

The door opened. She was dressed, too, in jeans and a black shirt. It washed out her complexion, made her look pale and ashen. The glow of their lovemaking was already gone from her face. She didn't speak.

He pressed his lips together. "I wish . . ." he began, then shook his head. "Never mind. I'm sorry. I didn't want to hurt you. Really. And I'd only hurt you more if I—" He stopped again.

She stared at him, unblinking.

There was no point. "I'll go." He turned, then hesitated. "Thanks."

"For the sex?" Felicity said bitterly.

"No, damn it! Not the sex. Not . . . just the sex. For every-thing. Just . . . being you." He swallowed. "I'm sorry. I'll go. I just want . . . Oh, hell, if—if there's ever anything I can do for you . . ."

She gaped at him.

"Never mind." He shrugged awkwardly, then, crushing his hat in his hands, he stumbled down the stairs.

She was a fool.

She was mortified. Horrified.

At her gullibility. At the wanton way she'd behaved. Every time she thought about it, about him—about loving Taggart Jones—her cheeks flamed, her gut twisted, she felt ill.

She wanted to pack up and run back to California, Iowa, her mother's womb! Anywhere far enough to get away from the confusing, taunting memories that haunted her.

But there was nowhere she could go to run away from herself.

Or from the love she still felt.

Perverse as it was, she found that when the mortification began to fade, when the horror subsided, when the anger began to seep out of her bones, the love—heaven help her—was still there.

She didn't know what to do about it. About him. There was nothing she could do, she told herself. He'd made his decision; he'd shoved her—and her love—out of his life.

"Chicken," she called him fifty times a day. "Coward."

But she never had a chance to say it to his face.

And then five days after Taggart had turned her life upside down, Orrin Bacon called.

"Ms. Albright? Been waiting to hear from you," he drawled. "About our little deal."

"I'm sorry, Mr. Bacon. I've been . . . distracted."

"Maybe you'd rather not do it. Lot of pressure on you. I'd understand if you were to change your mind."

But he wouldn't change his, Felicity knew. "I haven't changed my mind, Mr. Bacon. I'll do it."

"Do what, Ms. Albright? What exactly is this new trick you're going to learn?" He was chuckling. She could hear him.

Another day she wouldn't have done it. Another minute and she might have been more level-headed. But right now Felicity was reckless with need and anger and sorrow and longing. "I'm going to learn to ride a bull."

"Don't talk nonsense."

Just hearing her voice on the phone had stunned him. For a moment the words made no sense. When they did, his anger flared. He'd spent the last few days—ever since he'd walked out of her house—trying to put her out of his mind, trying to convince himself he'd done the right thing getting her out of his life.

And now here she was back in it again.

And spouting garbage about wanting to ride a bull?

"You've had women in your classes before," she reminded him. He cursed the fact that he'd told her so.

"Cowgirls," he said dampeningly. "Women who knew one end of a horse from the other."

"I know one end rather well, thanks to my acquaintance with you. Besides, this isn't about horses. It's about bulls."

He swore under his breath. "What's all this about, Felicity?"

"Orrin Bacon. I made a deal with him." She sounded downright breezy as she babbled on about old dogs and new tricks and him agreeing to let her teach Sam her way if she'd learn to do something, too. "So I said I'd learn to ride a bull." She made it sound like she'd agreed to learn to knit!

"That's idiotic!" Taggart paced as far across his living room as the phone cord would allow, then stomped back the other way again.

"It's necessary," Felicity countered. "So when's your next school?"

"Saturday. It's full."

"You can make room. Becky says you often do."

"You asked Becky?"

He and his daughter weren't on the best of terms. Ever since he'd told her flat out that he wasn't interested in her teacher, that she needed to keep her mind on her schoolwork and out of his love life, she had been talking to him in monosyllables—if at all.

"I did not ask Becky. She volunteered the information some time ago," Felicity said stiffly. "She says you make room for friends. And while I may not qualify as a 'friend' "—her voice twisted both the word and his gut "—I think you might allow a mere acquaintance in, especially your daughter's teacher."

"Damn it, of course you're a friend!"

"Am I?" Her tone was cool. "And here I thought I was just a roll in the hay."

He gritted his teeth. "You were never . . . ! Look, Felicity. There must be a thousand other things you could learn to do!"

"Of course there are, but this is the one I've agreed to. And I am not a chicken. What's the matter, Taggart? Are you?" she taunted.

"Damn you. No!"

"Well, then—?"

He raked a hand through his hair, then tugged it hard. "Oh, hell. All right."

She must have been out of her mind. That was all Felicity could think when she got up Saturday morning and realized that in an hour and a half she would have to turn up at bull-riding school.

She could call and back out, of course. It was what Orrin Bacon wanted. It was what Taggart wanted. In one sense, it was what *she* wanted. But she wouldn't do it.

Because more than she wanted to back out, she wanted to teach Sam the way he ought to be taught.

And because she wanted one last chance to see Taggart Jones—and make him see her. She'd felt this kind of determination only once before, when she had to convince her parents of her love for Dirk. It hadn't been easy. But she'd never regretted it.

She took Dirk's picture out of the drawer and looked at him. She hadn't been this scared since the day they got married. That had been a watershed moment, too. Everything in her life afterward had come as a result of that choice.

So it would—for better or worse—this weekend.

She brushed her thumb over Dirk's face. "Wish me luck," she whispered, and gave him a smile.

As always, he smiled back at her.

The cowboy hats were milling around when she got there. This time, though, she was one of them, wearing a new one she'd bought just yesterday. Tess Tanner had lent her some chaps, and old Mr. Eberhardt had come up with some spurs.

"Used to ride a few bulls myself in th'old days," he'd told her last night when he brought them over, folded inside the *Chronicle.*

Now she carried them to Taggart. The minute he looked up and saw her standing in front of him, all conversation in the room stopped. Did they all know? *What* did they all know? she wondered. Felicity ran her tongue along her upper lip, then held out the spurs. "Are these all right?"

Taggart took them from her. There was a low murmur of wonder that swept among the cowboys in the room. Taggart spun the rowels. He took his file and dulled one rowel, then another, carefully, deliberately. Then he handed them back to her.

Their eyes met. Felicity held herself very still.

"All right," Taggart said, eyes probing, querying, then finally sliding away. "Let's get started."

Eleven

He'd hoped she wouldn't show up. He'd known, of course, that she would.

It was the sort of woman Felicity Albright was. Stubborn, determined, committed. Crazy.

The same adjectives people had used to describe him when he resolved to keep Becky with him and take her down the road.

"A baby in a truck? You? By yourself?" He couldn't count the number of people who had gaped and shaken their heads at his foolishness. His own parents had told him he'd be better off to leave Becky with them. But he'd disagreed.

"A kid needs parents," he told them. "You were there for me when I was growing up. I'm gonna be there for Becky."

It hadn't been easy. Without Noah's and other cowboys' help at times, he couldn't have done it and he knew it. But he was glad he had. He had a relationship with his daughter that he never would have had if he'd left her with his folks.

She probably wouldn't have felt free to try to set him up with her teacher, for example. And he wouldn't be in the mess he was in right now.

How the hell was he going to teach Felicity—or anyone else, for that matter—how to ride a bull? He couldn't even think straight, let alone talk coherently.

The cowboys were shifting around restlessly in their chairs, waiting for him to get started. Felicity was watching him, too.

Just then, the door to the classroom opened and Becky poked her head in. "Daddy? You got a phone call at the house."

Taggart welcomed the reprieve. "Be right back," he said. With any luck she'd have come to her senses and left by the time he returned. He went up to the house.

"Taggart? Orrin here. She show up?" There was a note of mocking doubt in Orrin Bacon's tone.

No need to ask who he was talking about. Taggart straightened. His fingers tightened on the phone. "She showed up."

There was a second's surprised silence. Then, "With spurs on, no doubt." Orrin laughed.

"She has a pair, yes."

"Damn fool woman. You don't go lettin' her get hurt now."

"Injury is always a possibility in bull riding, Orrin. You know that."

"You ain't gonna let her on one, are you?"

"She has as much right to take my class as anyone else."

"But—but she's a *woman!*"

"I've noticed."

"She could get killed!"

"I hope not. I'll do my best to teach her how to be careful as well as how to ride. Why don't you come out and watch?"

"Watch? But what if—"

"I have to go, Orrin. I have a class waiting."

"But—!"

"Fish or cut bait, Orrin." Taggart banged down the phone and stalked back to the classroom, his mind whirling. He hadn't done much for Felicity Albright besides make her miserable since the day they'd met. He'd thought he owed her a night of loving. He'd been wrong. He didn't think he was wrong when he realized that he owed her this.

He walked straight over to her. "That was Orrin... checking up on you."

She looked nervous. "What'd you tell him?"

Taggart smiled grimly. "I told him to come out and watch you ride a bull."

It was the moment of truth.

Felicity stood on the metal rail of the chute and watched as the bulls were put in. In her mind she juggled a dozen thoughts, a thousand words. Put your feet even with the rope line when you start. Stay perpendicular to the back of the bull. Keep your body right over your feet. Angle your toes out. Pivot at the ankle, not the knee. Hug the bull with your calves. Keep your chin level. Don't drop your head. Be cool.

Only the last seemed to penetrate the fog swirling through her head. *Cool,* she told herself. *Be cool. Be calm. Be collected. Don't think. Just react.*

As if she'd be able to think, Felicity thought. The bull in the chute ahead of hers clanked loudly against the metal rails, blowing snot back over his shoulder and making the bell on his flank strap clatter as he kicked.

Tommy Hill, the high school boy slated for the ride, braced above the bull, hauled up on his rope once more, then lowered himself onto the bull's back. Half a dozen cowboys had already ridden—the advanced group, according to Taggart.

Now it was the beginners' turn.

Taggart, standing in the arena next to Jed McCall, who was going to pull the gate, was talking to Tommy as he eased down onto the bull's back. "Nice and slow," he was saying, his voice soothing. "Let him get used to you."

Felicity saw Tommy's hat bob once. The bull kicked against the metal. The railings clanged loudly once more. Tommy stood straight up again.

"It's okay. Go down again slow," Taggart said in the same calm, steady voice. "Good. Now, move up right into your hand. That's it."

Felicity could see Tommy wriggle forward cautiously.

The bull in the chute right below—*her* bull—snorted and kicked. She kept focused on Tommy.

"Ready," Taggart asked him.

Again Tommy nodded, one quick jerk. He let go of the rail and raised his arm, textbook perfect. Felicity could see the tension in his shoulders in the one moment of stillness before Jed pulled the gate and the bull exploded out of the chute.

It was over almost before it began. The bull spun sideways. Tommy slipped. His hand dropped. And he was on the ground and scrambling for the fence before Felicity could blink.

"Not bad for the first time," Taggart called. And then he looked at her.

She gulped.

"All right, Felicity," he said, his voice cool and professional. "Let's get you on this bull."

It was odd, she thought, how suddenly the world changed, shrank, and immediately everything around her became sharper, louder, clearer. The bull's back with its loose skin and rough hair. The pits in his one stubby horn. The smells of the resin on her rope and glove, of dirt and manure and chewing tobacco, of somebody's fruity bubble gum.

She was conscious of her knees wobbling. She sucked in a deep draught of air and hauled herself up to straddle the chute.

"Put on your glove," Taggart commanded.

She fished it out of her belt and pulled it on.

Taggart hauled himself up on the rail next to her. He was all business now. Steady. Firm. Dependable.

"Okay. Come on down." His voice had that same soothing tone he'd used with Tommy. Mindless, Felicity obeyed. She felt the loose warm hide of the bull spread beneath her. She felt the bite of the glove into the rope and instinctively rubbed it up and down, getting it warmer and tackier, the way real bull riders did. The way Dirk did with his cello bow.

Dirk.

You weren't supposed to think of anything irrelevant. You were supposed to stay focused, in tune. Taggart had said that. Felicity knew that.

And yet somehow the thought of Dirk gave her the edge she needed to clear everything else out of her head.

"I don't think about where to put my fingers," he'd said to her once when she was talking to him about a very difficult technical piece. "If I think about my fingers, I'll fumble all over the place. I'll hit the wrong notes altogether. I think about the music. I make music. I don't make notes."

"All set?" Taggart asked her. Her hand was wrapped. Her arm was up. Her calves clutched the sides of the bull.

I make music, Felicity thought. She smiled and drew in a breath. "Yes." Her voice was a whisper, but Jed heard her.

The gate swung open. Dirk fell away. Taggart fell away. Sam and Orrin Bacon and the rest of the world fell away.

It was just Felicity and the bull.

He gave a twist. A leap. A spin. She clung for one second. Two. Barely more. The world became a sea of color and motion, of power and thrust. Felicity clutched, meshed, balanced, swayed, flailed—was flung.

And then she had dirt in her mouth and her eyes, and felt the earth shaking beneath her as the bull's hooves barely missed her.

"Here!" Taggart yelled, and she scrambled toward him.

He hauled her up and onto the fence. "Okay?"

She lay half-over the fence, trembling, the world still spinning, all except the deep concern in his eyes just inches away.

"Okay," she said shakily. It had been like holding a tiger by the tail. Terrifying. Exhilarating. Awesome. She spat out a mouthful of dirt and grinned at him. "That's one." she said.

He admired her spirit, her determination, her grit.

He told his students he could teach them mechanics, but he couldn't teach them try. Felicity had try—in spades. She had everything he could ask for in a student—willingness, commitment, intensity.

He made up his mind to teach her the rest.

"That was a good move right there," he said when he critiqued her ride on the slow-motion video. "You were right where you were supposed to be." He forwarded the tape a few frames further. "See where your hand is here? You're starting to let it drop. When you do that, you pull yourself over to the side." He looked at Felicity.

She had a smudge of dirt on her cheek. Her braid was coming undone. She nodded, eyes intent on the video. He played the rest of the ride, including her spill face-first into the dirt. She grimaced, then laughed ruefully.

"You'll do better next time."

The smile she gave him nearly melted him in his boots. He steeled himself. "All right, guys ... and girl—" he grinned at her "—let's go."

She did do better next time. They were using pretty mellow bulls by rodeo standards. But any bull could give you a thumping, and Felicity lasted almost four seconds on the brindle bull she got on later that afternoon.

"You kept your arm up this time. But there, see where you stopped gripping with your calves?" He pointed. She nodded. The tape rolled on, showing her flying off and landing hard on her shoulder in the dirt. "That's what happens," he said matter-of-factly. "Back to work."

He wouldn't have blamed her if she'd called it quits. But when the cowboys limped out of the room minutes later, headed for the barn, Felicity limped with them.

Becky was impressed. She'd scarcely believed it when Ms. Albright got out of the car that morning wearing jeans and boots and a hat.

Becky knew she had the expression on her face that her grandpa said would catch lots of flies. She couldn't help it.

She'd been tempted to run back into the house and call Susannah right then, but she didn't want to miss a moment. She'd stayed right by Ms. Albright all day long. She hadn't gone to play at Susannah's that afternoon. She hadn't even gone down to Bozeman to spend the day with her grandparents, though they came up to get her. "I can't," she said. "I gotta stay here."

And watch. Supervise. Pray.

She didn't even stop to think that God might not be listening to a troublemaker like her. He couldn't be leading her on. He couldn't! He wouldn't bring Ms. Albright all the way out here just to grind her into the dirt before Becky's and Taggart's very eyes.

Would He?

Not the God Becky was praying to.

She'd worried quite a bit this past week, because her dad hadn't been exactly easy to get along with. He'd even yelled at her about staying out of his love life and minding her p's and q's.

Susannah said that was normal, but it hadn't felt normal to Becky. Now she thought that maybe Susannah knew what she was talking about.

Except that her father and Ms. Albright didn't seem to be all that happy to see each other. Was that normal? Becky wasn't sure.

She was sure, though, that Ms. Albright would be an okay mom. She decided that after the second bull ride.

"You okay?" Becky asked worriedly when Ms. Albright came limping back to the bleachers where she sat. "You're bleeding." She pointed to a scrape on Ms. Albright's chin.

"Am I?" Ms. Albright dabbed at the cut with her finger, then opened the water jug Taggart had sitting on the bleachers, poured a little water onto a tissue and washed the scrape. Then she fished in her knapsack, rooted around, and pulled out a Band-Aid.

Becky stared.

Misinterpreting the look, Ms. Albright hesitated, "You think it's sissy to put on a Band-Aid?"

Becky shook her head. "I like Band-Aids."

"Will you put it on for me?"

Becky took the Band-Aid and peeled off the paper covering. Then gravely, carefully, she covered the scrape with the sterile pad and smoothed the ends of the Band-Aid down flat.

"There," she said, studying Ms. Albright's chin with satisfaction. She smiled and looked up into her teacher's eyes. Ms. Albright smiled right back.

"Do you like carrots?" Becky asked suddenly.

Ms. Albright blinked, then wrinkled her nose. "Hate 'em."

Becky beamed. It was like they were sharing a secret, Becky thought.

She hoped they were.

By the time they had ridden their third bull, had listened to Taggart critique every ride, and then had gone back over what they'd learned, Felicity thought she might never get up out of her chair.

Every muscle in her body hurt. Every bone. Every sinew. Every ligament. Every brain cell, too, she was sure—provided she had any left.

"That's it, then," Taggart said at last. "See you tomorrow morning. 8:30."

There was a slow scraping of chairs, a few muffled mutters and groans. She was comforted to see that she wasn't the only one easing herself stiffly out of her chair. She pulled on her jacket, picked up her knapsack and headed for the door.

"Felicity." Taggart's voice stopped her. She turned. "I'll call Orrin tonight and tell him you've done it."

"I haven't done it."

"You've done enough. You don't have to ride eight seconds. For God's sake, pros don't always ride the full eight seconds!"

"Pros don't ride bulls like the ones I've been on, either." Though God knew they were rank enough for her. "I have to do it once," she said firmly. "Just once."

If she did, there would be no question in anyone's mind that she had ridden a bull. If she didn't... No, that didn't bear thinking about. She wasn't going to have gone through this for nothing.

"You don't—"

"Good night, Taggart. I'll see you tomorrow."

When tomorrow came, Taggart was willing to bet, she'd hardly be able to move her eyeballs. He half expected that she wouldn't show up. After all, she wasn't really trying to learn to ride a bull; she was just there to prove a point, and as far as he was concerned, she'd proved it.

But when he came around the corner of the barn the next morning, there she was.

She still had a bandage on her chin, and when she moved, it looked as if she was giving it some thought beforehand. But she was there.

He said, "Back again?"

She said, "And ready to go."

He gave them a pep talk first thing, then reviewed fundamentals. He talked to them about role models and showed a couple of brief video clips of some of the best bull riders in the business today.

"Learn from them," he said. "Watch them. Remember, it isn't the style you want to imitate. It's the mechanics. And the try. Go on now. The bulls are ready. But remember what I told you. It not only works in bull riding, it works in life."

Felicity, sitting in the front row, muttered something under her breath.

Taggart frowned. "What?"

She didn't answer, just lifted her gaze and stared challengingly up at him. Everyone else got up and left.

Some of them rode better than yesterday. Some rode worse. Felicity hit the ground on the second spin. She stumbled getting to her feet and fell again. The bull kicked her in the back.

Taggart heard the sound on the protective vest she wore. He shut his eyes and felt the bottom of his stomach drop. Felicity made it to the fence and scrambled over. Taggart breathed again. He was sweating and it wasn't even hot.

At noon Orrin Bacon showed up. He pulled into the yard in his dark green truck and sat for a minute, looking over the group as they ate hot dogs and bratwursts that Taggart's mother and Tess had fixed. He looked smug and supremely pleased until his gaze fell on Felicity. Then the satisfied smile disappeared.

He got out of his truck and crossed the yard. Felicity, who had been eating with a couple of the college boys, saw him and stiffened. Taggart saw her excuse herself and go to meet Orrin Bacon. It didn't take a genius to guess at the content of the conversation. Orrin asked a question. Felicity answered. Orrin's satisfied smile reappeared.

Felicity turned and came toward him. "We're not done yet, are we?"

Taggart wished he dared say yes. She looked like a stiff wind would blow her away. He didn't see where she was getting the strength. But he owed her honesty. "Not quite. Though from here on out, it's up to you. We're done with the critiquing. We've only got the jackpot left to do."

"What's that?"

"Anybody who wants to enter throws five bucks in the pot. We draw bulls and the guys ride. Just like a rodeo. Winner takes the pot. Two pots, actually, one for the beginners, one for the advanced. They don't have to be the full eight seconds. Just the best ride."

"Guys?" Felicity asked, eyes narrowing.

"Students," Taggart amended.

"So I can enter?"

"You could, but—"

"Good. I will." She gave Orrin a smile of her own.

"Who does the scoring?" Orrin asked.

"Noah," Taggart said. "And my dad." Sometimes he did it himself, but he didn't figure that would cut much ice with Orrin.

Orrin nodded. "All right, little lady. One more chance."

"Hey, Felicity drew Sunfish!"

"He ain't no beginner's bull!"

"Who put Sunfish in that round?"

"Whoa, wish I had 'im. That's half your points right there!"

"Gotta stick on 'im, though. Won't be easy."

"I can do it," Felicity said in a voice so small that not one of them heard her. It didn't matter. Not as long as she heard herself. "I can do it," she said again.

"You can do it," a small voice echoed beside her.

Felicity looked down. Becky stood looking up at her, eyes as green as Taggart's imploring and supporting her. Felicity smiled faintly. "You think so?"

Becky nodded, then reached out a hand and squeezed Felicity's fingers hard. "I know you can, Ms. Albright. If you want, I'll lend you my lucky spurs."

A weight seemed to lift off Felicity's shoulders. She smiled again, this time inside as well as out. "Thank you, Becky. I'd like that very much."

Taggart wanted to punch Orrin Bacon in the face.

He sat there at the top of the bleachers, fat and complacent, like some smug toad about to eat a bug. And Felicity was down behind the chutes, preparing to be the bug.

"Sunfish! For God's sake, who put Sunfish's name in the beginner's draw?"

"Oh, dear. I'm afraid I did," his mother said. "I didn't know you had a bull called Sunfish. I thought you meant Sunbonnet. You know, that nice little Angus bull?"

Taggart knew. It didn't help. He couldn't change things now. Everybody knew about Sunfish. Half of the guys envied Felicity for drawing him. The other half were glad it had been her and not them.

Taggart went back behind the chutes, uncertain what to say. He didn't want to spook her any more than she undoubtedly already was. The first riders were already going. He didn't pay any attention. He looked around for Felicity.

She was standing off in a corner by herself, not looking at the bulls or at the cowboys riding. She was in the midst of mayhem and yet seemed totally by herself. In a zone. He understood. He'd been there himself, looking for that center somewhere deep inside to hang on to.

Just then, she seemed to snap back to the present and look around. Her face was pale, but composed. It was a strong face, he thought now. Her bones were fine, but not frail. There was nothing ethereal or insubstantial about her.

"Felicity?"

She looked at him, seeing him for the first time.

He gave her a grave smile. "You can do it. Knock 'em dead."

When Sunfish blew out of the chute, he nearly ripped her arm right off. She didn't know how she managed to stay aboard, but she did. Maybe it was providence. Maybe it was grace. Maybe it was the extra suicide wrap one of the boys showed her how to take around her hand.

Whatever it was, she didn't ride pretty, but she rode.

She was whipped and spun, snatched and flung. But her calves stayed hard against Sunfish's sides. Her fingers stayed wrapped in the rope, and her overhead hand stayed high. She made a ride that was full of the clashes of cymbals and the pounding of drums. But in the end, it was music, not notes.

She heard yells and exhortations, cheers and shouts. Then she heard the loud blare of a truck horn that went on and on.

The buzzer! she thought. The buzzer! I've made it.

And then she couldn't figure out how to get off.

Wasn't that always the way? Nine times out of ten you got thrown off without wanting to, without even trying. And now, when you wanted—*needed*—to, you were stuck!

She wiggled her hand, trying desperately to free it, to shake off that last wrap. It held fast. She dropped her other hand, wanting to use it to free herself. But just as Taggart had said it would, brought down low, it threw her off-balance, caused her to slip sideways into the well of the twisting bull.

Jerked and snapped, flung and plunged, she slipped, slid, fell—but still couldn't let go. The bull's hooves caught her legs. Her arm was whipped and yanked, her body trapped. She saw Mace Nichols, who'd been doing the bull fighting, trying to move in close enough to free her. Jed and Taggart appeared out of nowhere, running, yelling, trying to move in, too. Desperately Felicity tried once more to wriggle free of the rope.

Suddenly Mace was next to her, shouldering his way in, catching hold of the bull with one hand and sliding his arm beneath her trapped one, levering it up and breaking the press of her weight against her hand hold.

Free, Felicity thought, free at last!

She fell to the dirt, stunned. Taggart bent over her. His face was ashen. "Are you all right?"

She knew he didn't mean that literally. He meant, *Are you alive?*

She was. Barely. She managed a smile. "Tell Orrin I know how to ride a bull."

The EMTs said she had some pretty impressive bruises. They said she had whiplash and that she was lucky she hadn't dislocated her shoulder and it wouldn't hurt to have an X ray just to check on her head.

They might have meant to see if she was concussed, but Felicity suspected they thought she was nuts and that had simply been a polite way of saying so. Maybe she was, but she was satisfied, too.

She was sitting on the table at the back of the classroom where they had taken her on a stretcher to poke and prod and check her over while the rest of the bull riding was still going on. But the minute they finished with her and opened the door, Orrin came directly in to see her.

The bluster was gone. "I gotta hand it to you, little lady," he said, shaking his head. "You got guts." He pumped her hand, making her grimace. "Oops. Sorry."

Felicity smiled a pained smile, and eased her hand out of his grasp. "It's all right."

"And you? You're all right?"

"A little sore, but I'll be fine," she assured him.

"Good. Good. Wouldn't want you missing any school, would we?" He shot her a quick look, one that said she'd won and he knew it.

Felicity smiled. "No," she said. "We wouldn't." Then, wanting it spelled out, she asked, "Does this mean you think you can trust me to know how to teach Sam now?"

Orrin Bacon smiled, too, a little self-consciously, then took a deep breath and nodded. "Said so, didn't I? I reckon I'll learn. I probably should say I'm sorry I pushed you to do this—" she opened her mouth to protest, but he held up a hand "—but I'm not. I admire you for it. You put your body where your mouth was, little lady. I'm proud to have you teach in our school. I'm proud to have you teach my son."

"Thank you," Felicity said faintly. "I'll do my best."

They shook hands again, more gently this time. Then Orrin Bacon left.

"I'm glad you're my teacher, too," Felicity heard Becky say soberly, and she realized that all this time the child had been sitting on a chair in the corner of the room. Now she came to stand next to the table where Felicity sat.

"You rode 'im good," she said. "Did my spurs help?"

"Oh, my, yes. Thank you."

"I'll lend 'em to you whenever you want."

"I . . . probably won't be riding any more bulls."

"Good. I don't want you to. I used to think I wanted to ride bulls like my dad, but after today, I don't think so." Becky still looked very worried.

"Not everyone gets hung up, Becky," Felicity said gently.

"But you did. You could've . . . you could've . . ." The little girl's lower lip quivered. Her green eyes were round and full of tears. "I'm glad you're not dead."

A faint smile lifted the corners of Felicity's mouth. "I'm glad, too."

"I wish . . ." Becky began, then her voice faded. She hugged her arms tightly across her chest. "I wish . . ." She tried again, then shook her head.

Felicity reached out and touched the little girl's cheek. They looked at each other. There were so many words, Felicity thought. None of which either of them dared to say.

Suddenly the room was filled with milling, whooping cowboys. "Hey, Felicity! Lookee here!" They crowded around her, beaming, and Becky got swallowed up in the throng. One of them handed Felicity a fistful of bills. "You won!"

She gaped at him. "Won? The jackpot?"

"You got a 65!"

"That's prob'ly 50 for Sunfish and 15 for you, but who cares?" Tommy Hill grinned at her.

"Not me." Felicity grinned, too. She felt giddy, disoriented, happy—and somehow desolate at the same time. Maybe she did have a concussion, after all.

"That'll teach ol' Orrin!" one of them crowed. "You better go out and celebrate! You deserve it."

"We all deserve it!" someone else yelled, and several more whooped their agreement.

"Of course," Felicity said, mustering what enthusiasm she could. "We will—with all this lovely money."

A general round of raucous cheers greeted that announcement. "Yea, Felicity!" And two of them made to hoist her onto their shoulders.

"Put her down!"

A sudden stunned silence filled the room. Taggart stood in the doorway, glaring at them, hands on his hips, green eyes flashing fire.

Slowly, with exquisite care, they put her down and stood staring at their boots.

"Back off," Taggart said tersely. "Give her some room. Better yet, get your carcasses out of here and let her rest." Felicity had never heard him sound this way before—harsh and angry, ready to fight.

"I'm all right," she protested, trying to lever herself off the table.

He ignored her. "Out," he said to the men. "All of you. Now."

They shuffled. They mumbled. They grumbled. They left.

All but Taggart—and Becky.

"You, too," he said to his daughter. "Grandma and Grandpa are waiting for you up at the house."

"But—" Becky's gaze flickered from her father to Felicity and back again, worriedly, warily, as if she didn't know what was going on.

You're not the only one, Felicity thought.

"Go on now," Taggart said in a gentler tone. "I need to take Ms. Albright home."

"You don't—" Felicity began.

But Taggart was walking Becky toward the door. "Please, Pard."

She looked up at him. Their gazes met. Whatever passed between them, Felicity couldn't see.

Then Becky nodded once. She turned and looked back at her. "'Night, Ms. Albright."

"'Night, Becky."

Becky started down the steps, then stopped and looked back at her father. "She doesn't like carrots, either."

They rode the whole way to town in silence. Only when they reached the highway and Taggart had the choice of turning south toward Livingston or taking Main Street toward Apple Street, did he speak.

"You sure I can't take you to the hospital?"

"I don't want to go to the hospital." She hurt enough. She didn't want any more poking and prodding of her body that night.

Taggart didn't argue. His lips set in a firm line, but he turned on Main, and the next thing Felicity knew, they were in front of her house. It was dark and she hadn't left a light on. Of course, Cloris had her porch light on. So did Alice. She just hoped they wouldn't come running out when they saw Taggart driving her home instead of her coming by herself.

"Thank you," she said tonelessly. She reached for the door handle, but he was out of the truck and coming around to open it for her almost before she'd moved.

Because he could hardly wait to be done with her, no doubt. Well, he could leave right now! She didn't know why he'd bothered to drive her home. Surely he didn't expect her gratitude to extend to a night in her bedroom! No, of course he wouldn't.

This was just some more stubborn Taggart Jones responsibility, she supposed. He needn't have bothered. She could get by just fine without his help. God knew in the long run she was going to have to. She'd accepted that over the past two days.

She couldn't control Taggart any more than she'd been able to control those bulls. He would do what he had to do, what he felt was right for him, and that was all she could ask. It hurt, but she knew that you survived hurt. She'd done it after Dirk's death. She'd do it again.

Taggart took her arm to help her down from the cab. She pulled away from him abruptly, hurting her shoulder as she did so. She sucked in a sharp breath. "I can move on my own!"

Taggart muttered something under his breath, but stepped back, stuffing his hands into the pockets of his jeans, and let her get down by herself. She was already stiffening up again, and she limped as she went up the walk. She thought perhaps he'd leave if she didn't acknowledge him, but instead he followed her up the walk.

She rounded on him. "You don't have to trail after me! I'm fine. Leave me alone!" She was perilously close to tears. Apparently knowing she'd survive and having to face it were two different things.

Was it the sudden depletion of adrenaline, maybe? The letdown after she survived her hang-up on the last bull ride? Or was it because she knew that for all Orrin Bacon would be singing her praises now and welcoming her into Elmer Elementary School, she also knew she couldn't stay.

It was like the old westerns always said—the town wasn't big enough for both her and Taggart Jones.

"I want to talk to you," Taggart said. He didn't come any farther, but he didn't leave, either. He stood at the foot of the steps, looking up at her.

"Now?"

He nodded.

Felicity gripped a porch pillar. "Fine. Talk."

He glanced around as if he could see the curtains twitching. "I'd like to come in."

Felicity gave her best imitation of an indifferent shrug. Whatever he had to say couldn't be any harder to listen to than everything he'd already said. "Suit yourself." She turned and opened the door, going in. Taggart followed her.

Felicity turned on the light, then turned to face him. "Forgive me if I don't offer you coffee, but I don't think you'll be staying that long."

"I'd like to," he said quietly.

She stared at him, jolted.

Was he expecting to go to her bedroom then? Her eyes narrowed suspiciously.

Taggart shifted from one foot to the other, looking less remote now than ill at ease. He still didn't speak, though. Neither did Felicity. She couldn't think of a thing to say.

Finally he ran his tongue over his upper lip and swallowed. "I know it isn't worth much," he told her, "but I wanted to tell you...I was proud of you." Green eyes met hers, deep and intense.

Felicity knotted her fingers in front of her. "Thank you."

"You've got guts."

"Thank you again."

His mouth twisted. "So, after a fashion, does Orrin—being willing to trust you with his kid. Even though you proved yourself, he's still taking a risk."

She didn't know what to say to that, so she didn't say anything.

Taggart dug his toe into the faded rug underfoot. "Made me think," he said, "how everybody else has guts but me." He slanted her a quick glance.

Felicity stared at him, breath drawn in, mute.

He sighed. "I talk a good fight," he told her. "You heard me." Once more a corner of his mouth lifted self-deprecatingly. "All that stuff about determination and willingness to risk and try. And I can do it on a bull. But I don't do so good in real life."

Which meant . . . what? Felicity didn't say a word, only waited.

Taggart ducked his head and stared at the floor for a long moment, then raised his eyes once more to meet hers. "What happened with Julie scared me spitless. I felt I'd let her down bad, and maybe I did."

"You don't have to explain."

"Yes, I do, because it's what I used it as an excuse not to try again. Like if you'd got thrown and never got on another bull."

"It's hardly the same thing."

"It's exactly the same thing. All that stuff I spouted about bull riding being like life. Well, it's true. Only I never managed the connection myself. You did. You got up and got on again. Didn't you?" His eyes bored into hers.

Felicity ran her tongue over her lips, then nodded slowly.

"You tried again," he said heavily. Then he gave her a look that was both hungry and wistful. "I'd like to try again, too."

Felicity felt like her tongue was welded to the roof of her mouth. Was he saying what she'd hoped for so long that he'd say? Or was she, in fact, concussed?

"Maybe I should have that X ray after all?" she said faintly, still disbelieving. Her knees wobbled and she gripped the back of the overstuffed chair.

Taggart closed the distance between them and put his hands on her arms, his grip gentle, but strong, supporting her. A rueful smile quirked the corner of his mouth. "You aren't concussed. Everything you're hearing is true. I love you, Felicity. I've loved you for a long time and it's scared me to death." He gave a shaky laugh. "I'm still scared, but I can't be any more scared than you were when you got on those bulls."

Lifting a hand, she touched his cheek. "I was terrified," she admitted.

"Yeah, well, so am I. And you ought to be to, 'cause I'm asking you to marry me."

Her eyes widened. Her heart leapt. She stared up into his gaze, hardly daring to believe his words. But she could see the truth there in his eyes. She saw his heart, his soul—his love— waiting just for her.

"Well," he said impatiently and more than a little apprehensively when she didn't reply at once. "What do you say?"

Felicity blinked. She sniffed. She managed a watery smile and winced as she raised her arms to loop them around his neck and draw his head down for a kiss.

"Yes," she said. "Oh, yes."

"What *is* that smell?"

Taggart knelt naked straddling Felicity's equally naked thighs as he rubbed the soothing salve into her back. He rued the bruises he saw forming. He bent to kiss each one. "Horse liniment," he said. "Bag balm. Oil of wintergreen. Camphor. A little turpentine." He grinned. "I really don't know what it is. My sister dreamed it up. She's trustworthy."

"Do I get to meet your sister?"

"Not today. Today you're staying right here." He straightened up and began to knead her shoulders.

Felicity sighed. "Heaven," she mumbled and tried to roll over, but he kept her trapped between his legs. She was smiling. He was glad. He wanted her to keep smiling for the rest of her life. He leaned down and feathered a row of kisses along her spine.

She shivered. "Taggart," she protested.

"Hmm?" He nuzzled her neck.

"You're insatiable."

"Uh-huh."

He was—but not just for her touch. For all of her. Forever. Mind and body. Heart and soul.

He'd come so close to losing her. Not just to Sunfish— though the memory of her hung up on that bull would haunt him the rest of his days—but to his own reluctance to risk, to love again. After his divorce from Julie, it had seemed smarter—safer—not to.

Why bother to try when you might only get hurt? Why dare when you might just get shot down?

When was love worth the risk it would take?

The sight of Felicity's tense, white face as she'd settled down on Sunfish this morning had answered that question for him.

First it had made him want to stop her. *You don't need to do this!* he'd wanted to say.

But the look she had given him froze the words in his throat. There had been a steadiness in her gaze, a centerness that he'd seen in other bull riders. One he'd found, when he was riding, inside himself. He recognized it, understood it. But there had been something else, too. There had been a connection—a link between them, a trust that he didn't think he imagined.

It was as if she had been saying, *I can do this because you taught me how, because I know you believe in me.*

And sensing that trust, he'd answered with his eyes. *I do. I'll help you.*

Now he hoped to God that, when it came to love and marriage, Felicity would help him, too.

She tried once more to turn beneath him, and this time he let her. They looked at each other a long time. Touched. Smiled.

The connection—the trust, the love—was still there.

"Come to me, Taggart," Felicity whispered then, and held out her arms to him. "I must be insatiable, too."

He sighed and settled into the warmth of her embrace. He should have been sated, loving her the way he had. But he wasn't. He didn't think he ever would be. He ought to let her rest. She had to be stiff and sore.

But when he said so, she just shook her head. "I'm fine. Must be that miracle salve you're using."

"I love you."

"Show me."

He smiled, no proof against her touch and the flame of love in her eyes. "Maybe I will," he murmured, feathering kisses in her hair, "just once more."

Felicity smiled. "Just once?"

"Well, maybe more than once." He kissed her mouth. And then, with exquisite care, he set about showing her how much she meant to him.

He drew her on top of him this time, then waited, letting her settle over him and take him deep inside. And then their gazes, their bodies, their very hearts and souls were locked together.

Two made one.

He still wasn't sure he deserved this love she was offering, but if it was his for the asking, he wasn't saying no.

He was saying yes, please, forever. And ever. Amen.

"When will you marry me?"

It was morning now. Late morning. His truck was still parked in front of her house. No doubt the neighbors would already have spread the news. If they didn't, the secretary at Elmer Elementary certainly would have, after Felicity had called at six-thirty to tell her she wouldn't be in that day, she was just a little too stiff and sore.

And not entirely from bull riding, either, though she didn't mention that.

"As soon as you want," Felicity said now, nibbling along the line of Taggart's jaw.

"Tomorrow?"

"In a hurry, are you?"

"Damn right. Besides, ol' Cloribel and company will want you to make an honest man out of me."

"I will," Felicity promised. "But maybe we should wait till the weekend. I have to teach tomorrow."

Taggart smiled thinking about how her students would react to the news. "Wonder what Becky will say."

"I don't," Felicity said dryly.

He laughed. "Neither do I. She'll say I told you so." He rolled over onto his back and pulled Felicity on top of him. "When we get married, you'll have your daughter in your class. Think you can handle that?"

Felicity smiled lazily. "I'm looking forward to it. But I'm looking forward to having her in my family even more."

"She's going to be thrilled." And Taggart, remembering Becky's imploring looks, her desperate intensity, knew that *thrilled* didn't even begin to cover it.

"She can be my bridesmaid," Felicity said. "I'll make our dresses."

"She'll like that." An understatement if there ever was one. Taggart smiled, imagining the two of them—the women in his life—walking down the aisle to meet him. Then a grin split his face. He laughed.

"What?" Felicity demanded.

Still grinning he rolled her in his arms. "I was just wondering if we'll be able to talk her out of wearing her spurs!"

* * * * *

*That's not all from this part
of the West! Look for Jed's story,
COWBOY PRIDE, coming from
Silhouette Desire in November 1996.*

Miss Rebecca Kathleen Jones

requests the honour of your presence

at the marriage of her father

Taggart William Jones

to

Felicity Jane Albright

daughter of Mr. and Mrs. Joseph Morrison

at 11:00 a.m.

on Saturday, November 18th

Elmer Community Church

Elmer, Montana

reception immediately following at the community hall

black tie optional   no spurs

The first book in the exciting new
Fortune's Children series is

HIRED HUSBAND

by *New York Times* bestselling writer
Rebecca Brandewyne

Beginning in July 1996
Only from Silhouette Books

Here's an exciting sneak preview....

Minneapolis, Minnesota

As Caroline Fortune wheeled her dark blue Volvo into the underground parking lot of the towering, glass-and-steel structure that housed the global headquarters of Fortune Cosmetics, she glanced anxiously at her gold Piaget wristwatch. An accident on the snowy freeway had caused rush-hour traffic to be a nightmare this morning. As a result, she was running late for her 9:00 a.m. meeting—and if there was one thing her grandmother, Kate Winfield Fortune, simply couldn't abide, it was slack, unprofessional behavior on the job. And lateness was the sign of a sloppy, disorganized schedule.

Involuntarily, Caroline shuddered at the thought of her grandmother's infamous wrath being unleashed upon her. The stern rebuke would be precise, apropos, scathing and delivered with coolly raised, condemnatory eyebrows and in icy tones of haughty grandeur that had in the past reduced many an executive—even the male ones—at Fortune Cosmetics not only to obsequious apologies, but even to tears. Caroline had seen it happen on more than one occasion, although, much to her gratitude and relief, she herself was seldom a target of her grandmother's anger. And she wouldn't be this morning, either, not if she could help it. That would be a disastrous way to start out the new year.

Grabbing her Louis Vuitton totebag and her black leather portfolio from the front passenger seat, Caroline stepped gracefully from the Volvo and slammed the door. The heels of her Maud Frizon pumps clicked briskly on the concrete floor as she hurried toward the bank of elevators that would take her up into the skyscraper owned by her family. As the elevator doors slid open, she rushed down the long, plushly carpeted corridors of one of the hushed upper floors toward the conference room.

By now Caroline had her portfolio open and was leafing through it as she hastened along, reviewing her notes she had prepared for her presentation. So she didn't see Dr. Nicolai Valkov until she literally ran right into him. Like her, he had his head bent over his own portfolio, not watching where he was going. As the two of them collided, both their portfolios and the papers inside went flying. At the unexpected impact, Caroline lost her balance, stumbled, and would have fallen had not Nick's strong, sure hands abruptly shot out, grabbing hold of her and pulling her to him to steady her. She gasped, startled and stricken, as she came up hard against his broad chest, lean hips and corded thighs, her face just inches from his own—as though they were lovers about to kiss.

Caroline had never been so close to Nick Valkov before, and, in that instant, she was acutely aware of him—not just as a fellow employee of Fortune Cosmetics but also as a man. Of how tall and ruggedly handsome he was, dressed in an elegant, pin-striped black suit cut in the European fashion, a crisp white shirt, a foulard tie and a pair of Cole Haan loafers. Of how dark his thick, glossy hair and his deep-set eyes framed by raven-wing brows were—so dark that they were almost black, despite the bright, fluorescent lights that blazed overhead. Of the whiteness of his straight teeth against his bronzed skin as a brazen, mocking grin slowly curved his wide, sensual mouth.

"Actually, I *was* hoping for a sweet roll this morning—but I daresay you would prove even tastier, Ms. Fortune," Nick drawled impertinently, his low, silky voice tinged with a faint accent born of the fact that Russian, not English, was his native language.

At his words, Caroline flushed painfully, embarrassed and annoyed. If there was one person she always attempted to avoid at Fortune Cosmetics, it was Nick Valkov. Following the breakup of the Soviet Union, he had emigrated to the United States, where her grandmother had hired him to direct the company's research and development department. Since that time, Nick had constantly demonstrated marked, traditional,

Old World tendencies that had led Caroline to believe he not only had no use for equal rights but also would actually have been more than happy to turn back the clock several centuries where females were concerned. She thought his remark was typical of his attitude toward women: insolent, arrogant and domineering. Really, the man was simply insufferable!

Caroline couldn't imagine what had ever prompted her grandmother to hire him—and at a highly generous salary, too—except that Nick Valkov was considered one of the foremost chemists anywhere on the planet. Deep down inside Caroline knew that no matter how he behaved, Fortune Cosmetics was extremely lucky to have him. Still, that didn't give him the right to manhandle and insult her!

"I assure you that you would find me more bitter than a cup of the strongest black coffee, Dr. Valkov," she insisted, attempting without success to free her trembling body from his steely grip, while he continued to hold her so near that she could feel his heart beating steadily in his chest—and knew he must be equally able to feel the erratic hammering of her own.

"Oh, I'm willing to wager there's more sugar and cream to you than you let on, Ms. Fortune." To her utter mortification and outrage, she felt one of Nick's hands slide insidiously up her back and nape to her luxuriant mass of sable hair, done up in a stylish French twist.

"You know so much about fashion," he murmured, eyeing her assessingly, pointedly ignoring her indignation and efforts to escape from him. "So why do you always wear your hair like this . . . so tightly wrapped and severe? I've never seen it down. Still, that's the way it needs to be worn, you know…soft, loose, tangled about your face. As it is, your hair fairly cries out for a man to take the pins from it, so he can see how long it is. Does it fall past your shoulders?" He quirked one eyebrow inquisitively, a mocking half smile still twisting his lips, letting her know he was enjoying her obvious discomfiture. "You aren't going to tell me, are you? What a pity. Because my guess is that it does—and I'd like to know if I'm right. And these glasses." He indicated the large, square, tortoiseshell frames perched on her slender, classic nose. "I think you use them to hide behind more than you do to see. I'll bet you don't actually even need them at all.''

Caroline felt the blush that had yet to leave her cheeks deepen, its heat seeming to spread throughout her entire quivering body. Damn the man! Why must he be so infuriatingly perceptive?

Because everything that Nick suspected was true.

* * * * *

To read more, don't miss
HIRED HUSBAND
by Rebecca Brandewyne,
Book One in the new
FORTUNE'S CHILDREN series,
beginning this month and available only from
Silhouette Books!

MILLION DOLLAR SWEEPSTAKES

No purchase necessary. To enter, follow the directions published. For eligibility, entries must be received no later than March 31, 1998. No liability is assumed for printing errors, lost, late, nondelivered or misdirected entries. Odds of winning are determined by the number of eligible entries distributed and received.

Sweepstakes open to residents of the U.S. (except Puerto Rico), Canada and Europe who are 18 years of age or older. All applicable laws and regulations apply. Sweepstakes offer void wherever prohibited by law. This sweepstakes is presented by Torstar Corp., its subsidiaries and affiliates, in conjunction with book, merchandise and/or product offerings. For a copy of the Official Rules (WA residents need not affix return postage), send a self-addressed, stamped envelope to: Million Dollar Sweepstakes Rules, P.O. Box 4469, Blair, NE 68009-4469.

SWP-M96

Silhouette's recipe for a sizzling summer:

* Take the best-looking cowboy in South Dakota
* Mix in a brilliant bachelor
* Add a sexy, mysterious sheikh
* Combine their stories into one collection and you've got one sensational super-hot read!

Summer Sizzlers

MEN OF *Summer*

Three short stories by these favorite authors:

Kathleen Eagle
Joan Hohl
Barbara Faith

Available this July wherever Silhouette books are sold.

Look us up on-line at: http://www.romance.net

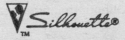

TM

SS96

FORTUNE'S Children™

New York Times Bestselling Author
REBECCA
BRANDEWYNE

Launches a new twelve-book series—FORTUNE'S CHILDREN
beginning in July 1996 with Book One

Hired Husband

Caroline Fortune knew her marriage to Nick Valkov was in
name only. She would help save the family business, Nick
would get a green card, and a paper marriage would suit both
of them. Until Caroline could no longer deny the feelings Nick
stirred in her and the practical union turned passionate.

MEET THE FORTUNES—a family whose legacy is greater than
riches. Because where there's a will…there's a wedding!

Look for Book Two, *The Millionaire and the Cowgirl,*
by Lisa Jackson. Available in August 1996 wherever Silhouette
books are sold.

You're About to Become a *Privileged Woman*

Reap the rewards of fabulous free gifts and benefits with proofs-of-purchase from Silhouette and Harlequin books

Pages & Privileges™

It's our way of thanking you for buying our books at your favorite retail stores.

Harlequin and Silhouette—
the most privileged readers in the world!

For more information about Harlequin and Silhouette's PAGES & PRIVILEGES program call the Pages & Privileges Benefits Desk: 1-503-794-2499

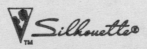

Silhouette®

SD-PP156